The
FRESH
NEW
FACE
of
Griselda

The
FRESH
NEW
FACE
of
Griselda

JENNIFER TORRES

Little, Brown and Company
Hachette Book Group
1290 Avenue of the Americas, New York, NY 10104
Visit us at LBYR.com

First Edition: October 2019

Little, Brown and Company is a division of Hachette Book Group, Inc. The Little, Brown name and logo are trademarks of Hachette Book Group, Inc.

The publisher is not responsible for websites (or their content) that are not owned by the publisher.

Library of Congress Cataloging-in-Publication Data
Names: Torres, Jennifer, 1980– author.
Title: The fresh new face of Griselda / by Jennifer Torres.
Description: First edition. | New York ; Boston : Little, Brown and Company, 2019. | Summary: After her father's landscaping business fails and the family loses their house, sixth-grader Griselda Zaragoza follows her sister's example and begins selling Alma cosmetics while hiding her changed circumstances from friends.
Identifiers: LCCN 2018050074| ISBN 9780316452601 (hardcover) | ISBN 9780316452595 (ebook) | ISBN 9780316452588 (library edition ebook)
Subjects: | CYAC: Poverty—Fiction. | Loss (Psychology)—Fiction. | Sisters—Fiction. | Moneymaking projects—Fiction. | Cosmetics—Fiction. | Family life—Fiction. | Hispanic Americans—Fiction.
Classification: LCC PZ7.1.T65 Fre 2019 | DDC [Fic]—dc23
LC record available at https://lccn.loc.gov/2018050074

ISBNs: 978-0-316-45260-1 (hardcover), 978-0-316-45259-5 (ebook)

Printed in the United States of America

LSC-C

10 9 8 7 6 5 4 3 2 1

For Alice and Soledad, my favorite sisters,
and Anthony and Mark, my favorite brothers

CHAPTER ONE

Beautification to my mind is far
more than a matter of cosmetics.
—LADY BIRD JOHNSON

No one is coming to the door, but not because no one is home. Inside the apartment, a baby howls over the gentle murmur of a lullaby.

This is hopeless.

"Let's just go," I tell my big sister, Maribel. "She's too busy."

The two of us barely fit on the porch. We had to step over a fern and shove aside a stroller just to get to the door.

Maribel ignores me. She is not giving up. She

presses her lips together, narrows her eyes, and stares at the door as if, by focusing hard enough, she can will the person inside to open it.

She breathes in deeply through her nose and tries the doorbell again. "Is this thing even working? Did you hear it ring?"

I don't answer—first, because she isn't really asking me, but also because it's hard to tell. The baby's sobs have turned into big gulping hiccups, and those are the only sounds I can say for sure I hear coming from inside the apartment's thin walls.

Maribel huffs. She stops pressing the doorbell and knocks instead, sharp and insistent. *Bam, bam, bam.*

I give up on leaving the porch anytime soon and sit down next to the fern. A maidenhair. There's a frayed blue ribbon tied around the pot and a small, yellowing card that reads *Welcome, Baby!*

The tips of the fern are brown and beginning to curl, so I unscrew the top of my water bottle and pour out the last warm drops. There's only enough to dampen the top layer of soil, but it might help, and anyway, it's the best I can do.

I toss the empty bottle into a cardboard box

filled with recyclables in the corner of the porch, then slump forward and rest my chin on my knees.

"We've been out here forever, Mari. She's not going to answer. Can we just go ho—" I stop myself. "Can we just go back?"

"You could have stayed with the car," Maribel says, without taking her eyes off the door.

"I couldn't have stayed with the car—it's like a million degrees outside."

It is, too. Fall is just a few weeks away— according to the calendar at least. But during these last days of August, breezes still blow so hot and dry they make your eyes burn. Beads of sweat tickle on their way down my neck and under my T-shirt.

Yet even in her stiff, plum-colored blazer, Maribel doesn't seem to be sweating at all. Her makeup satchel slips down her shoulder, and she hefts it up again.

Knock, knock, knock.

"You're just going to make her mad."

"She's going to be *happy* to see me," Maribel argues, through a too-sweet grin. "She"—*knock*— "just"—*knock*—"doesn't know it yet."

She's lifting her fist to knock again when the

door creaks open. Not more than a few inches, just enough to see a woman's red-rimmed eye blink at us. Enough to startle me. I slide a little farther away.

Maribel lowers her arm, steps back, and squares her shoulders. Her candy-apple smile glistens as she tilts her head and says, "Good afternoon. It's a pleasure to meet you. My name is Maribel." She pauses to tap her name badge with a flawlessly manicured fingernail. "And I'm here with Alma Cosmetics, the Soul of Beauty."

Her voice goes up when she says *soul*, the way a bird trills when it sees the sun rise.

She actually thinks this is going to work. I want to look away but can't. My ears go hot, even though if anyone should be a blushing bundle of nerves right now, it's Maribel, not me.

But I don't think Maribel remembers what nervous feels like. I mean, if she ever knew to begin with.

Holding a baby in one arm, the woman opens the door a little wider. She looks from Maribel to me and shakes her head. "This is...not a good time," she whispers, then starts to close the door as the baby begins snuffling.

But Maribel is unstoppable. Instead of walking away, she takes a step *closer*. Part of me wishes I had stayed in the car after all.

"Those," Maribel says, leaning in toward the lady as if she's about to tell her a secret, "are the longest eyelashes I have *ever* seen. Listen, I totally get it: You don't have time, and I don't want to keep you. But can I just ask, what brand of mascara do you use? I mean, I'm an Alma girl, one hundred percent, but for that kind of volume..."

And then the woman laughs.

It's a thin laugh that sounds as if it might break apart like glass if we aren't careful. But still. She's laughing.

"Mascara?" She looks down at her T-shirt where a splotch of baby drool is slowly spreading over her shoulder. "I call it a good day if I manage to brush my teeth."

Maribel takes another step closer. "Get *out*. Are you telling me those lashes are... *natural*?"

The woman rolls her eyes and moves the baby onto her other hip.

"All right, all right, don't get carried away," she

says. But she's still smiling. Her eyelashes even flutter a little. She takes her hand off the door.

"I'd invite you in, but I'm a mess, the place is a mess, and he"—she pauses, turning to nuzzle the baby's nose with hers—"is a mess. Not to mention overdue for a nap."

It's as if Maribel doesn't hear any of it. She holds out her arms. "Why don't you let my sister, Griselda, hold him for a minute—babies love her—and I'll show you a few samples? Just for fun?"

"Mari!" I protest.

She turns to me and mouths, *Get up!* then repeats aloud, "Babies *love* her."

The door opens wider still.

"No pressure or anything—we've made all our sales for the day," Maribel continues. "It's just that we were on our way out when I saw the stroller and heard the baby and thought, 'There's someone who might appreciate Dewy as Dawn, our new replenishing moisturizer.' It's a real miracle worker. And if you don't mind my saying so, you look like you could use some pampering."

Some of what Maribel says is true, anyway.

We were on our way back from the mall when Maribel took a detour. She was exactly one order short on her sales goal for the Alma Cosmetics item of the month. Sell thirty jars of Dewy as Dawn replenishing moisturizer and she would win a special prize and cash bonus. Sale number thirty, Maribel had decided, was buried like treasure somewhere in this apartment complex, and we weren't going to leave until she found it.

We walked up and down stairs, and back and forth across breezeways, Maribel's eyes darting from door to door. "Fifteen minutes," she muttered to herself. "Get me in the door and give me fifteen minutes."

I didn't know what she was looking for, and she wouldn't stop to tell me. I could hardly keep up.

"How about this one?" I said, pointing to an apartment, trying to be helpful. "At least we know there's someone home." The woman inside was stirring something in a skillet—I could just see her through the gaps in the blinds. I couldn't tell what she was cooking, but from the smell that drifted out the window, I guessed it had onions and green peppers.

Maribel scowled and kept walking. "With food on the stove? Get serious."

She finally stopped when we came to the apartment with the stroller parked in front. I couldn't see what made it so different from any of the others, but Maribel said, "This is it. Fifteen minutes."

And after the lady finally invites us in, that's almost exactly how long it takes Maribel to make her sale.

By the time we leave the apartment, she and her new customer are hugging goodbye as if they've known each other since forever—while I pry the end of my braid out of the baby's chubby fingers. I give him back to his mom, her face freshly moisturized. Replenished. Dewy, some might say.

"Bye-bye," I whisper to the baby, waving. He waves back, his hand opening and closing like a sticky, slobbery lobster claw.

"I'll see you again in a few weeks," Maribel calls from the sidewalk. "When it's time to reorder!"

I can't believe she pulled it off. Even for Maribel, it was kind of amazing.

We walk back to the car, and I wait on the passenger side for Maribel to peel off her blazer and unlock the door. It's late afternoon, the warmest part of the day, when heat spills down from the sinking sun and also seems to rise up from the baking asphalt.

"How did you know?" I ask.

"Know what?" she says, rummaging through her bag for the keys.

"That it would work?" I say. "That she would finally open the door? That she wouldn't just tell us to get lost?"

Maribel shrugs. "It's not that hard if you know what you're looking for. Stroller on the porch—she planned to go out but the kid wouldn't cooperate. Dead plant—too distracted to even water it. No time to take out the recycling." Maribel finds the keys and lets us into the car. "It was the same way with Mom when you were a baby. That lady wasn't going to turn down a grown-up conversation. She *definitely* wasn't going to turn down the chance to give her arms a break."

I move the shoebox I had left on my seat and climb inside, careful to keep my legs lifted a few inches off the hot upholstery.

Maribel digs a notepad and booklet out of her

satchel. She opens the notepad and turns to a dog-eared page. "Thirty jars of moisturizer, plus the extra lipstick, puts me over five hundred dollars for the month. That should be..." She taps a pen against her teeth. "A seventy-five-dollar cash bonus and..." She flips through the booklet, frowns. "A 'rose-gold watch with *glaaaamorous* crystal accents,'" she reads. "Great. *Just* what I need."

"Rose gold sounds nice."

Maribel drops the booklet on top of the cup holder between our seats. She checks the rearview mirror and backs out of the parking space. "I guess. Maybe I can sell it."

"Too bad you had to lie for it."

"Geez, I didn't *lie* to her, I just...made her feel like herself again. Anyway, are you trying to tell me that Alma's new miracle moisturizer *didn't* leave her face looking as dewy as the dawn?" Maribel steers onto the street. "As dewy as the very *dawn?*" she says again, this time grabbing my shoulder and shaking it for emphasis.

I wriggle away from her. "Keep your hands on the steering wheel." Then I pick up the booklet, wishing a dab of lotion was all I needed to feel like myself again.

Sales Rewards, it reads on the cover. *With Alma Cosmetics, your business is a thing of beauty!* I open it. Inside, there are pictures of watches and bracelets, purses and scarves—prizes my sister can earn if she sells enough makeup. The biggest picture of all is of a saleswoman smiling in the driver's seat of a silvery-purple convertible. She wears a plum-colored blazer just like Maribel's, and her caramel-brown ponytail flies out behind her, blown back by the wind on an invisible open road. *The Soul of Ambition!* the booklet exclaims. *Accelerate your career with Alma's car program, an exclusive reward for associates averaging $3,000 a month in sales.*

Three thousand dollars a month. I wonder how many jars of lotion that is. How many lipsticks. How many candy-apple smiles and "Pleasure to meet yous" standing outside a stranger's doorway. It seems like an impossible number.

Then I look up at my sister, one elbow hanging out the rolled-down window, her shining black eyes focused on the street ahead. If anyone can do it, it's Maribel.

"*What?*" she says, sensing my stare.

I look away, out my own window. "Nothing."

"Whatever. Check inside my bag—in the side pocket," she says. "There should be a little box."

I twist around and reach into the back seat where she had left her satchel.

"This?"

Maribel glances over and nods. "Keep it. For dealing with the kid. Totally sealed the deal."

I open the box and shake out a tube of lip gloss, carnation pink with teensy flecks of gold. I twist off the applicator brush and sniff. Smells like strawberries, only sweeter than the real thing. The label on the bottom says this shade is called Once Upon a Time.

"It's from the new Fairytale Collection," Maribel explains. "Flatters everyone. You can try it out for the first day of school."

"Right. I get it. 'Once Upon a Time.'"

But this doesn't feel like a beginning. And the story we're stuck in the middle of? It's definitely not a fairy tale.

I drop the lip gloss into my cup holder, then set the shoebox on my lap. I lift open the top, and there they are, the shoes Mom had sent Maribel and me to buy at the mall, all ready for the start of sixth grade tomorrow.

Plain and white.

I sigh. Louder than I mean to.

Maribel nudges me with her elbow. "Geez, seriously. They're not that bad."

C⁓

Mom and Dad gave me my name, of course. My real name. Griselda Zaragoza.

A strong name.

A family name.

A name like an ugly stepsister.

A name like a gurgle.

A name that starts with lumps and bumps and ends in sharp, jagged edges.

But the one Maribel gave me—her name literally means *beautiful*, by the way—turned out to be worse.

It was after recess on my first day of kindergarten, and I was crying in a bathroom stall. Ms. Encinas, the recess supervisor, was just outside the door, trying to coax me out.

"Griselda? Sweetheart? Will you open the door? Or just tell me what's wrong? I *really* need you to use your words right now." Her voice was soft, as downy as my naptime blanket. But I could hear a hint of impatience in it.

"All right. Well, I'm going to see if I can find some extra help. But I'll be right back, okay? I promise."

Part of me was relieved when Ms. Encinas went away. The more she asked what was wrong, the smaller I felt, and the harder it was to tell her. I wondered if she had gone to get the principal. Or my teacher? Maybe she was going to call my mom.

I waited. Besides my sniffles, the only sounds were the *drip, drip* of a leaky faucet and the quiet whir of the ventilation fan until a voice called into the bathroom.

"What are you *doing* in there?"

It was worse than the principal.

"It's like I told you, Maribel. Your sister's been crying in there for the past ten minutes. I don't know what's wrong and I can't get her to come out. I thought maybe she would feel better if you were here."

The soles of Maribel's shiny black Mary Janes *click-clacked* over the blue-green bathroom tiles and stopped in front of my stall. Light from the ceiling panels winked off her toes.

Thwap, thwap. The door rattled when she knocked.

"Geez, get out. Right now."

G.Z. for Griselda Zaragoza.

Gee Zee, only the more Maribel said it, the more she slurred the initials, and the more it came out as *Geez*, so that she sounded annoyed every time she said my name.

As if she were asking, *Oh, geez, what now? Oh, geez, what were you thinking?*

As if she were rolling her eyes.

As if she were tearing her hair out.

Even when she had no reason to. Only that day, I guess, she kind of did.

"Geez, come *on*. Open the door. I'm missing math, you know." It was her first day of seventh grade. Mom had told her to look out for me, but she probably wasn't expecting that Maribel would have to leave class to rescue me from a bathroom stall.

Ms. Encinas interrupted. "Maybe you should take it a little easier on her, Maribel. First days can be tough for anyone."

"Geez, come out!"

"Can't," I croaked.

"What?"

I cupped my hands around my mouth and yelled into the bathroom door, "I can't!"

"What do you mean, you can't?"

"It's locked."

"So unlock it."

I held my breath. The faucet *drip, drip, dripped*, and finally, I admitted, "Don't know how."

The first day of kindergarten was also the first time I had ever spent more than a few hours apart from my mom. All summer long, she had been preparing me to tie my shoelaces by myself, to punch a straw through a juice box by myself, to make friends by myself.

But until that morning at recess, I had never been inside a bathroom stall by myself. It seemed easy enough, and it was—at first. I figured out how to lock the door behind me. But not how to get back out again. I didn't know what to do and was too embarrassed to say so.

Maribel groaned and the door shivered again as she hit her head against it.

"Oh, *Geez*. Okay, fine. So just crawl under."

No way. I shook my head, even though Maribel couldn't see me. The floor looked too dirty and damp, and I didn't want to ruin my first-day-of-school dress.

Suddenly, Maribel's head appeared under the door. I yelped and jumped backward, nearly falling into the toilet. Seconds later, she had slithered into the stall and was standing with her hands on my shoulders.

"Geez," she said. "When are you going to stop being such a baby?"

"*Easy*, Maribel," Ms. Encinas warned.

Maribel flipped open the lock and nudged the door open with her hip. I started to step out, but before I could, she closed and locked the door again.

"Huh?"

"Like this," Maribel said, demonstrating. *Flip open and nudge.*

The door swung open. She pulled it closed and locked it. "Try it."

Flip open and nudge.

"Again."

I unlocked the door and pushed it open with my shoulder.

"That's it. You got it now?"

I sniffed and nodded and swiped my hand across my eyes.

When the two of us emerged for the last time, Maribel smoothed her skirt and checked her hair in the mirror, tucking a loose strand behind her ear. She stepped over to the sink, yanked two paper towels from the dispenser, and dampened them under the faucet.

"Come on," she said. "You're fine." She dabbed my face and straightened my headband.

"I mean it, Geez. You're fine," she said again in a whisper, squeezing my hand. "I'm going back to class now."

Ms. Encinas patted my head.

"*Geez*? Is that what your family calls you?" She shrugged. "Well, Griselda *is* an awfully big name for such a little girl, I suppose," she said, taking my hand and leading me out of the bathroom. "Let's get you back to kindergarten, Geez."

I kept expecting Maribel to complain to our parents about what a baby I had been, how she had to miss class because of me. But she never told them one single thing about it.

CHAPTER TWO

I have been very happy with my homes, but
homes really are no more than the people
who live in them.
—NANCY REAGAN

There are two ways back to the house, and all I want right now is for Maribel to choose the longer one—the one that won't take us down West Mariposa Avenue, the street we used to live on. The street we don't live on anymore. But Maribel is not the sort of person who wastes any time taking the scenic route, not without a good reason.

"Didn't Mom tell us to pick up some milk?" I ask, hoping to give her one.

Maribel shakes her head. "What? No, she said she'd get some later tonight. She was going to stop at the grocery store anyway, remember?"

We drive a few more blocks, and I try again.

"Shouldn't we get some gas, though? Mom's going to be mad if you bring the car back empty."

"There's *still* half a tank, and anyway it's *still* my car."

I should have known better. Bringing up the car was a mistake. There's no coming back from, not with someone as stubborn as Maribel. All I can do now is tell her the truth. "I don't want to see the house, Maribel. Can we go the other way? *Please?*"

"Geez," she says, pulling down her sun visor. "You have to get over it."

Minutes later, like I knew she would, my sister turns onto West Mariposa Avenue. I don't slap my hands over my eyes, but I want to. Instead, I open the Alma rewards booklet again, not really focusing on the pictures, just concentrating hard on not noticing the houses on either side of the ash-lined street. Especially one house. My house. The house that *used* to be mine, I mean, from the time I was born until last spring when we lost it.

I know what that means, of course—that we had to move out of our house because Dad's landscaping company went out of business and my parents couldn't make the payments anymore. But *lost* still seems like the wrong word. It doesn't make sense that a house can be *lost* when it's still right there at the very edge of my vision.

"It's weird," Maribel says quietly, after making the last turn on our way to Nana's house, where we've been living for the past four months. "How it looks exactly the same, you know? From the outside, I mean. All your roses are still there and everything. Looks like someone's taking care of them."

I nod but don't lift my eyes just yet, worried I might accidentally look into the rearview mirror and see my old garden. Seeing it makes me feel the way I did that time a soccer ball flew into my stomach during PE. Stunned and gasping. I *know* the house isn't ours anymore. But I only *feel* that when I see it.

I turn to the back cover of the prize booklet. *The Spirit of Success!* it screams in bold, swooping, purple letters.

Are you between the ages of 12 and 19? Join Alma

as a *Junior Associate and help us celebrate the Fairy-tale Collection, our new makeup line especially for teens and tweens. Just sell 500 tubes of Fairytale Collection lip gloss, and you could win $5,000, plus the chance to become the Fresh New Face of Alma Cosmetics!*

Under the words is a picture of a girl—older than me but younger than Maribel—holding a bouquet of purple balloons, enough balloons to lift her off the ground and carry her far, far away. From the giggling look on her face, I'd guess she had been skipping along, not a worry in the world, when she found the balloons just floating there. And the longer I stare, the more I think she looks exactly like the kind of girl who is *always* finding stuff and never, ever losing it.

I set the booklet on top of the shoebox and fold my hands. It doesn't matter what Maribel says. I know our house can't possibly look the same anymore, not without us living in it.

Mom and Dad had said things would be back to normal soon. That we would live with Nana only long enough for Maribel to finish high school. That we'd find a place of our own before I started sixth grade. I believed them. Like I always did.

But Maribel's graduation was months ago, and unless we moved into a new house *tonight*, my parents weren't going to be able to keep their promise. With Dad living six hours away, trying to find a new job in Los Angeles, it seems even more unlikely that they ever will.

Maribel pulls into Nana's driveway and parks next to an overgrown riot of a camellia bush. Brittle brown petals from last year's flowers flutter down onto the windshield. This season's buds are already fattening on the branches, about to explode into pink blossoms.

Convincing Nana to prune the bush back was impossible, but I had tried to explain to her about raking up the dead blooms at least. How they could spread petal blight if you don't.

But she didn't care if there were brown spots on her flowers.

"That tree isn't entering any beauty pageants," she had said. "It'll do just fine on its own. Always has."

That's exactly how she feels about everything else in her garden. If you can even call it one. A garden means order. A garden is a long-term plan.

Nana's yard is random and wild. She buries all her kitchen scraps out there: eggshells and apple cores, coffee grounds and carrot tops.

"No, no, no," she said once, when she caught me about to throw away a banana peel. "Save it for the garden."

She says all that trash is good for the soil, and every so often, some of what she buries grows. Garlic shoots sprout near a pineapple crown. Potatoes have taken root next to a leafy head of celery. And a patch of mint is slowly devouring the whole yard, inches at a time. Some mornings the smell of it, cool and clean, drifts in through the kitchen window.

Nana's always telling us not to stand too still out there, that the mint might swallow us, too. It's a silly joke, and I've heard it about a million times. But when I look at that mint patch, growing thicker and greener, the idea doesn't exactly seem impossible.

Yet, even though it's nothing like the one Dad and I had planted at our old house, Nana's garden wouldn't bother me so much if it weren't for the toilets.

There are six of them: two on the front porch, the rest standing in a row along the fence. Some people choose flower *beds* or flower *pots*. But Nana chose toilets. Most of them started off inside her house, hauled outside only when they cracked or she couldn't scrub the porcelain clean anymore.

One came from a neighbor. "You're not throwing that away, are you?" Nana had yelled across the street when she saw them carrying it to the curb for the garbage collector.

She hates to see a thing go to waste if it might be even a little useful, and to her, almost anything is at least a little useful—whether it's a brown banana peel or an old toilet.

So the neighbors brought theirs to Nana's garden, where she filled it with soil and geraniums.

I can't stand those toilets.

But I can't ignore Nana's geraniums, wilting under the scorching sun. They can't help where they're planted, after all. I set down the shoebox and lip gloss and unwind the hose while Maribel gathers her makeup bag, her blazer, and all those Alma booklets and brochures.

Next door, Logan Johnson is lifting grocery bags out of his mom's trunk. He's in my grade at school, and I have known him since always.

"Hey," he says, saluting me with a gallon-size jug of milk. Logan has curly, blackish-brown hair that's always falling over his forehead and into his eyes.

"Hey," I say, lifting the hose nozzle back at him.

He blows a puff of air up at his forehead, and I can see his face clearly for just a moment before his hair flutters down again. "Ready for school tomorrow? Your mom said you have Ms. Ramos, too."

I nod. I used to spend almost every weekend with Logan—playing handball against his garage door, or practicing free throws, or feeding Magdalena, his pet garter snake—when we went to Nana's house for Sunday breakfast. But ever since we moved in with her, I hardly ever see Logan except for times like this, when we just sort of run into each other.

"We could walk to school together?" He says it like a question.

Maribel whistles, just loud enough to send a warm flush across my cheeks.

I try to ignore her. "Maybe. But my mom might drive me." She usually does on the first day of school. One of her little traditions.

Logan shrugs. "Okay. See you there." He reaches into the back of his mom's car to grab another shopping bag.

"*We could walk to school together,*" Maribel repeats in singsong on her way up Nana's front porch steps. "How *cute*. Good thing I gave you that lip gloss, huh?"

I look over my shoulder to see if Logan has heard her. His back is to us, on his way inside with the groceries.

I twist the faucet, aim the hose at Maribel's sandals, put my thumb over the nozzle, and spray.

"Geez!" Maribel screeches, hopping on one foot to avoid the rush of water. Then she stops, squeezes her eyes shut, and breathes out slowly. She shakes a few droplets off her hand and steps through Nana's door as if nothing has touched her at all.

Behind me, I hear Logan's laugh and then the clatter of his screen door closing. After I water the geraniums and pull a few dead flowers off the old camellia, I coil the hose, dry my hands on my shorts, and gather my things to go inside, too.

Mom is sitting at Nana's kitchen table reading

a magazine. She puts it down when I come in and looks up with big, hopeful eyes. "There she is." She sees the shoebox. "Soooo…let's see! What'd we pick out?"

Pick doesn't seem like the right word. The shoe store didn't have much of a selection, at least not in our price range. I shouldn't complain. I know that. But I don't feel like showing off the shoes for Mom as if Maribel and I had just come home from a shopping spree.

"Just shoes," I mumble.

"Oh." She droops like the geraniums.

"I mean, they're fine. Sorry. I'm just…sweaty. And tired. Thanks for the money. Do you want the change back?" There isn't much of it.

Mom smiles a sad half-smile and shakes her head, so I take the coins with me to the bedroom I'm sharing with Maribel.

The room had been Mom's when she was growing up—hers and Tía Carla's. I almost can't believe Mom was the one who had chosen the daisy-chain wallpaper or the lavender curtains. That she had picked out the matching lamps, with their polka dot shades and white ruffle trim. What's not so hard to believe is that Nana hadn't changed a thing after all these years.

I leave the lip gloss on my nightstand with the school supplies Mom and I bought at the dollar store last week and drop the shoebox against the wall, next to my open suitcase.

As soon as we moved in, Maribel had decorated her side of the room with photos of her friends and pictures she'd clipped from magazines. The dried-up corsage from her junior prom rests on top of the desk next to her graduation tassel and the twinkling tiara from her quinceañera.

She had left two dresser drawers and half the closet empty for me to put away my clothes. But since Mom and Dad had promised we wouldn't be staying very long, I never unpacked.

Then, the longer we stayed, the sooner I thought we must be leaving. Now I can't help feeling as though if I finally *do* unpack, it means we've given up. Nana's house is really where we live now, not just a place we're staying for a little while. So every week, after Maribel and I do the laundry, I fold my clothes and put them right back in my suitcase, rcady to move to our real home whenever my parents figure out where that is.

Most of my stuff—my books and music, my nail polish and gardening gloves, the rainbow tangle of thread that my best friend, Sophia Arong, and I used to braid and knot into bracelets—is still packed away in cardboard boxes, somewhere in Nana's garage.

Besides my clothes, all I've brought inside from my old bedroom is my collection of First Ladies of the United States teacups. I wasn't sure they'd be safe in the garage. So, cushioned in bubble wrap and crumpled-up tissue paper, they're packed inside a box and stashed under the bed. All except for one of them. That one, the first in my collection, sits on the windowsill, the only clue that this room is mine.

I've had that cup since Nana and I found it at a yard sale when I was four. It's the color of the heavy cream Mom pours into her coffee, and I remember thinking when Nana bought it for me that, even with its chipped gold rim, it was the most elegant thing I had ever held. Like something a princess would sip tea out of.

On one side of the cup, in an oval frame, is a portrait of a woman who looks as if she could be a queen. Or at least she did to me, when I was four. Her hair is thick and cinnamon brown like mine, but it's teased into a cloud around her face. She wears diamond earrings and a golden dress with sleeves that fall over her shoulders like lily petals. Her smile is warm but faraway.

On the walk home, Nana had told me that woman's name was Lady Bird Johnson and her husband was the thirty-sixth president of the United States.

From then on, every yard sale with Nana became a quest. We never knew where—or when—the next piece in my collection might turn up. We found Nancy Reagan in a bargain bin full of souvenir ashtrays and coffee mugs. Abigail Adams buried under a pile of tea towels and oven mitts. My point is, sometimes you have to search.

I have eighteen teacups so far. Lady Bird Johnson is not the most valuable in my collection, or even the prettiest. But it reminds me of home, of that feeling I used to have with Nana, that beautiful things could be anywhere—hiding where I least expected, waiting to be discovered.

I take the teacup and spill the change from the shoe store inside. Then I hold it between my palms for a few moments before putting it back on the windowsill for the night.

CHAPTER THREE

I am who I am, and I will continue to be.
—Pat Nixon

Sunlight peeks through the gap between Mom's lavender curtains. It glints off the gold rim of my Lady Bird Johnson teacup. The first day of sixth grade. I had woken up on my own, without the alarm clock, like I always do on days when something important is going to happen. But I don't get out of bed right away. Serving us breakfast in bed on the first day of school is another one of Mom's traditions—although Maribel always says it wasn't a tradition until *I* started school.

Maybe it's babyish—my sister would say so—but

after everything that's happened, I'm looking forward to Mom's first-day breakfast. To *something* being the same as it used to be. Last Saturday, when Dad made his weekly check-in call, I asked him if he would drive up to Nana's house so he could be here, too. He said he would try. I didn't believe it, though. Not really. I don't think he did either, and anyway, I'm not surprised he isn't here this morning.

My sister is still asleep in her bed against the opposite wall. Her arms are flung over her head, but even when she's sleeping, she seems so sure of herself. Unstoppable.

I wonder if Mom will bring Maribel breakfast in bed, too. It's not the first day of school for her, since Maribel isn't in school anymore, a subject she and Mom have been fighting about most of the summer.

A floorboard squeaks under the hallway carpet. I pull Nana's crocheted afghan up around my neck and turn toward the wall, pretending to be asleep so Mom can wake me.

Then I listen more closely. These footsteps aren't like Mom's, not quiet and creeping. There's no clink of dishes on a breakfast tray. I open my eyes, sit up, and see Nana silhouetted in the bedroom doorway.

"Mija?" she whispers. "Are you awake?"

"I'm awake. But where's Mom?" I lean forward, trying to look beyond Nana, into the hallway.

Her shoulders drop. "Your mami left early to help Tía Carla open the salon for one of those too-important-for-business-hours clients of hers. Ven, I have breakfast ready for you in the kitchen."

Just then, Maribel jolts upright and runs a hand through her hair. "Wait, she didn't take *my* car, did she? I need it. I have Alma appointments scheduled all over town today."

Nana grimaces. Maribel groans.

"What about Grandpa's car?" I suggest.

My grandfather died when I was still a baby. I used to think that if I closed my eyes and tried hard enough, I might remember his voice. His smell. The color of his eyes. Something left over in my memory. But it never works.

Nana keeps his big, gold Crown Victoria parked on one side of the driveway. She doesn't drive it very often, but she washes it every Saturday morning, no matter what.

"Sí," Nana agrees. "If you take Griselda to school, you can borrow your grandfather's car for the day."

"Fine," Maribel says. She yawns and drops back onto her pillow.

Nana checks her watch. "Ándale, then—both of you better get moving if you want to be on time."

I stretch, swing my legs off the bed, and pull a pair of faded gray jeans out of my suitcase. I grew over the summer, and the pants are sort of short now. But if I cuff them at my ankle, it almost looks as if that's the way they're supposed to fit.

Next, I unfold a sleeveless button-up shirt, the same violet-blue of wild forget-me-nots. I haven't worn it all month, half hoping that when I finally put it on again, it might feel like something new. Like last year, when Mom left a sundress with tags still attached hanging off my bedroom door for the first day of fifth grade.

It was that spring, the school year almost over, when Maribel and I got home and found Mom and

Dad waiting for us on the living room sofa. Something was wrong. It wasn't just that Dad was home so early. There were times when projects at work made him late for dinner every night for weeks on end, but other times were slower: mornings when he was still in pajamas, dunking crumbly pink polvorones in his coffee when I left for school, and afternoons when he was already at home, weeding our garden when I got back. Last spring was one of the slower times. Maybe it had gone on for a little longer than usual, but I hadn't thought much about it.

Instead, what made everything seem wrong that day was how still Mom and Dad were, as if they were posing for an old-fashioned camera, the kind where, if you moved, it ruined the whole picture. No one was saying anything. No one was even looking at me. Outside, in the cul-de-sac, an ice-cream truck played "Pop Goes the Weasel." I remember hoping that, whatever Mom and Dad had to tell us, they would hurry up and finish before the truck drove away. I wanted an orange Creamsicle. No kidding, that was the biggest thing I had to worry about back then. I *thought*.

Finally, Maribel walked into the living room

and sat in an armchair opposite our parents. I followed her, relieved someone had broken the eerie quiet spell and actually *done* something, had unfrozen us.

"Is it your bid, Dad? What happened? Did you get the contract?"

I had no idea what Maribel was talking about, or how she knew what was going on. Dad dropped his head. Mom looked at him, then looked at us.

"No," she told Maribel. "He did not get the contract." Then she took a deep breath and let it out slowly, as if she were blowing out candles on a birthday cake, only she knew none of her wishes would ever come true. She clapped her hands on her knees and looked at me and then my sister. "Griselda, Maribel, listen. We are losing the house. We need you to know this is not forever—and everything's going to be all right." It was her gentle but steady voice. The voice that said, "Pay attention," but also, "Don't panic." It was her voice for scraped knees and waking up from nightmares. "It might not seem like it at first, but everything is going to be just fine. Everything *is* fine—but we're going to move in with Nana for a little while—"

Maribel interrupted. "So that's it? You're just going to stop trying? Game over?"

Dad got up off the couch, ran his hands through his thick black hair, and walked over to the window. "Maribel, I owe money to three different banks. No nursery within a hundred miles will sell me anything on credit anymore. The truck needs new brakes, and I can't pay for those either. So, unless you won the lottery and forgot to tell us, then, yes. That's it. Game over."

"For how long?" she demanded.

"At least through the end of your senior year," Mom said. Her voice was as steady as a heartbeat. *Pay attention. Don't panic.* "We want you to graduate with your class. After that, I'm not sure—we need to sort some things out. Dad needs to find some more work.... You know we're very lucky we have family we can turn—"

"*Dad* has to find some more work? Why can't *you* get a job? What, little Griselda can't survive without Mami at home to fix her an after-school snack every day?"

Dad wheeled around. "Maribel, you will not talk to your mother—"

Mom raised a hand to hush them both. She closed her eyes and swallowed. When she finally spoke, her words were quiet and clipped.

"Of course I'll try to get a job. Of course I *have* been trying. But Maribel, it's not that simple."

Maribel looked away and threw herself back into the armchair.

I was trying to keep up, but I didn't understand and no one was explaining anything. We were moving in with Nana. Dad was looking for a job. Mom was looking for a job, too. Neither of them could find one. Maribel blamed me for...something.

"We're losing the house?" I finally blurted. "Where is it going?"

"Oh, Geez." Maribel got up and stalked out.

We started packing the next weekend.

One by one, I took my teacups, delicate as egg-shells, off the shelf above my desk. Stamped on the bottom of each was a quote—something wise or clever a First Lady had said or written. I read every word as I rolled the cups in bubble wrap, but nothing the First Ladies had to tell me was very much help.

I emptied my closet and swept all the barrettes

and hair elastics out of my bathroom drawer. I went to the garage where I had stored some summer-blooming flower bulbs—dahlias and ranunculus and begonias. I didn't know where I would ever plant them. Or when. But, just in case, I wrapped them in dishtowels and packed them up, too.

Dad left his truck at the mechanic's and drove Mom's station wagon down to Los Angeles. It's where he grew up, where his brothers, my tíos, still live, and where he thinks we have a better chance of starting over.

Now whenever Mom needs a car, she takes my sister's. If I were Maribel, I guess I'd want to win that silvery-purple convertible, too.

CHAPTER FOUR

Happiness is not where you think you find it....
So many people poison every day worrying
about the next.

—Jacqueline Kennedy

Mom would never have given me coffee. One of
the reasons I used to like staying over at Nana's
house—before we were staying here permanently,
I mean—is that she pretends she doesn't hear when
Mom says coffee will make me jittery or stunt my
growth, and not to pour me any.

When I sit down at the kitchen table, Nana fills
my mug, half with coffee and half with cream, then
sprinkles cinnamon and sugar on top. She brings

me a bowl of oatmeal and half a concha, my favorite kind of pan dulce, from the Mexican bakery around the corner. She walks there every morning, even when it's raining, and is back at the house before the rest of us even wake up.

I eat the oatmeal first, leaving a pile of raisins behind in the bowl (because Nana also pretends not to hear when I tell her that raisins are awful, so wrinkled and chewy). Then I break off a piece of concha, letting the crumbly topping fall over my fingers, and dip it in the coffee. It soaks it up like a sponge. The perfect mix of bitter and sweet.

Nana glances nervously at the clock on the microwave when Maribel's blow-dryer roars to life in the bathroom. But I'm not worried. Maribel is never late.

"Do you have everything you need, mija?"

"Think so."

I have my backpack from last year, the school supplies laid out on the nightstand, and of course, my new shoes. I look down. There isn't anything wrong with them, really. They're clean and new, bright and white. But so plain.

I have an idea.

"Actually, Nana, maybe there's one more thing I need. Can I use some of your wrapping stuff?"

She starts to open her mouth as if she's about to ask why, but changes her mind. "Ándale," she says. "But you better hurry. You don't want to be late on your first day."

Nana always opens her presents slowly and cautiously, painfully careful not to rip or tear the wrapping. It doesn't matter how much we tease or complain; she never rushes. And all the paper, all the ribbon, all the bows and bags she thinks are too nice to just throw away she keeps on a shelf at the top of the hallway closet.

Maybe some of it is useful after all. I drag a chair over from the kitchen and climb up to try to find what I need.

Under a square of silver wrapping that I recognize from Nana's birthday last year, I find a long piece of ribbon the color of marigolds. It's frayed at the ends, but only a little.

I hop off the chair and hurry to the bedroom, where I snip the ribbon in half with a pair of scissors. Each piece is just long enough to weave over my shoelaces and tie in a neat bow. I wish I had time to check the whole outfit in a mirror, but the shoes feel better, at least, with a little more color.

"Geez, you're going to make us late!" Maribel calls.

I grab my backpack from off the floor, hold it open against my nightstand, and rake in pens and pencils and erasers. "Coming!"

Maribel is waiting for me at the door, holding the keys to Grandpa's car in one hand and in the other, a pig-shaped gingerbread cookie with its ear bitten off. Her hair is braided and coiled up in a bun. Her mouth looks as if she's just finished a grape lollipop.

"New item of the month?"

She smacks her lips. "Sugar Plum," she says. "Let's go."

We lean down for Nana to kiss our foreheads on our way out the door. Outside, Logan is sitting on his front porch steps, poking at a spiderweb with a twig. He drops it and stands when he sees us.

"I heard your mom drive off earlier, so I knew she wasn't giving you a ride. I waited—just in case you want to walk together after all?"

"That's okay. Maribel's giving me a ride."

She elbows me in the ribs. *"Geez!"*

"Ouch! *Okay.*" I turn to Logan. "Sorry. Do you want to come with us?"

"Plenty of room," Maribel adds, patting the side of the Crown Victoria. "This thing is basically a tank."

Logan picks up his backpack and scrambles down the steps. Maribel unlocks the doors. I sit up front with her, and Logan climbs in back.

It's not that I don't like him. Logan is pretty much family. I mean, even before we moved in with Nana, I saw him more often than any of my actual cousins, and I can't even remember a time when I *didn't* know him. Mom's photo albums are filled with pictures of Logan and me dressed as Red Riding Hood and the Big Bad Wolf for Halloween, of us diving for candy when the piñata broke at my birthday parties, and of bright blue raspado syrup dripping off our chins and staining our shirts when it was summertime.

I even sort of miss him, which is a strange thing to feel, I mean, considering we've been living next door to each other for months now. But that's the problem. I never told anyone at school what happened with the house last year. But it's not like I can hide it from Logan. Every time I see him I hold my breath and clench my jaw and wonder when he's finally going to ask why we're living with Nana, or how long we're going to stay, or when my dad is coming back.

The thing is, I don't know the answers to any of those questions, and I don't want to say so out loud. So whenever Logan came to the door this summer, I told him I was busy. And every time I heard his basketball bouncing on the driveway, I just stayed inside.

But on the way to school, Logan doesn't ask why we're living at Nana's, or where Dad is, or even why we're riding with Maribel in Grandpa's enormous Crown Victoria and not with Mom.

Instead, he leans forward and asks, "You haven't seen Magdalena, have you?"

"Oh, no." I twist around to face him, the seat belt straining against my neck. "She didn't get out again, did she?"

He brushes his hair out of his eyes. "She got out again."

Magdalena is completely harmless—unless you're

a guppy, obviously. She's even sort of beautiful in a way, deep forest green with yellow stripes.

Nana doesn't think so.

"Well, you better find her fast. You remember what happened last time, don't you?"

Logan shudders.

He had invited me over to watch Magdalena eat her lunch one Sunday last year. Only, when we got to his bedroom, she wasn't in her aquarium. His mom said he must have left the lid open, but he swore he closed it. We emptied Logan's drawers and tore through his closet trying to find her. We checked in all his shoes and even turned all his pockets inside out, but Magdalena had completely disappeared.

Logan had dropped a guppy in her bowl. "Maybe she'll come back when she's hungry." We went to go shoot free throws in his driveway.

Logan had made twelve shots in a row. He was going for number thirteen when we heard a shriek from Nana's yard. The ball dropped. We ran over—Logan's mom three steps behind us—to see what had happened.

I had never seen Nana so upset. She was screaming—she was even cursing—but none of us could understand what was wrong. Finally, Ms. Johnson took her by both wrists and got her to calm down enough to explain. Sort of.

Nana pointed at Logan, then to one of her toilet planters. "Get it out of there," she growled.

"Get what? Wh-where?" Logan stammered. He looked from Nana to his mom, to the planter, and back to Nana again. And then the color drained from his cheeks. He finally understood. "Oh."

He bit his lower lip, walked over to the toilet, and crouched down for a closer look. Gently, he pushed aside stems and leaves and flowers. "There you are."

I shake my fist like Nana had that afternoon. "If I ever, *ever*, find that thing in my garden again, I'll bring her back home myself," I roar.

"In pieces!" Logan and Maribel shout together.

We had all laughed until we cried that day. Even Nana, after the surprise finally wore off.

We're all laughing again as Maribel pulls over to let us out of the car half a block away from school. "This close enough for you guys?"

"It's fine." Logan and I click open our seat belts in unison.

I unlock my door, but Maribel puts a hand on my shoulder before I can open it. "Hey."

I turn to face her. "Yeah?"

"Have a good day and all that," she says. "Okay?"

"Okay," I say. I push the door open and step outside.

"Thanks for the ride," Logan says as she drives away.

"Thanks for waiting." I really mean it. I'm glad he's here. Because as long as I was laughing with Logan, I could stop thinking about my too-short jeans or my plain shoes or how different everything is from the way the first day of sixth grade was supposed to be.

CHAPTER FIVE

You just don't luck into things as much as
you'd like to think you do. You build step by
step, whether it's friendships or opportunities.

—BARBARA BUSH

Ms. Ramos got married over the summer. She's
Mrs. Ramos-McCaffrey now, and she starts class
by passing around postcards from her honeymoon
in Spain: A dreamy cathedral that looks like the
drip castles I used to make with seawater and sand
at the beach. A flamenco dancer with a rose behind
her ear and a whorl of red ruffles around her feet. A
green reflecting pool, surrounded by myrtle trees.

As we pass the postcards from desk to desk,

Mrs. Ramos-McCaffrey hands out sheets of blank white paper and asks us to write and illustrate post-cards from our own summers. "Think of this as a chance to catch up with one another *and* to warm up those descriptive writing skills. We'll go around and share when you're finished."

Great.

I blink at the empty sheet of paper in front of me. I try to avoid talking in class to begin with, and the idea of talking about the past few months makes me want to crawl underneath my desk and hide.

I have nothing to draw. Nothing as beautiful as Mrs. Ramos-McCaffrey's postcards, anyway. How do I draw the vacations we didn't get to take? The strawberries in my old garden that are someone else's to pick? The flower bulbs I never planted?

My heart beats faster as, all around the room, my classmates start whispering about beach houses and roller coasters and summer camps and science museums. I tap my pen against my cheek. I have nothing to add to the conversation. *My parents can't pay for any of that stuff anymore,* I think, but don't say. *The most interesting thing I did this summer was water the toilets in Nana's garden.*

Before I've had a chance to think of anything to write about, Mrs. Ramos-McCaffrey announces that it's time to share. "Who wants to start us off?"

Logan raises his hand. He holds up a drawing of a skinny green snake with yellow stripes. "This summer," he says, "I trained Magdalena—she's my pet snake—to play hide-and-seek."

"Oh?" Mrs. Ramos-McCaffrey asks.

"She's better at the hiding part."

Everyone laughs.

"Thank you, Logan. Next, let's hear from…" Mrs. Ramos-McCaffrey looks down at the roll sheet. "Zachary. Zack—do you go by Zack?—tell us about your summer."

Logan's postcard has given me an idea. I have just enough time to scribble out a drawing and a few short sentences before Mrs. Ramos-McCaffrey calls my name four students later. Luckily, Nana's camellia is the botanical version of a big, messy scribble.

"This summer, I helped my nana take care of this wild old camellia bush she has growing near her driveway. It…um…it still needs a lot of work." I remind myself to look up, to enunciate, to *project* like Mom is always reminding me. "But at least it's a start."

I say the last sentence like it's a question. *At least it's a start?* Mom hates that. "Are you telling me, or are you asking me?" she would have said. "Say it like you *mean* it."

I don't relax my shoulders until Mrs. Ramos-McCaffrey says, "Very nice," and moves on to Ava without asking any follow-up questions.

"Thank you for sharing such lovely memories," she says, after everyone has had a turn. "If you think about it, social studies is sort of like the memories of a whole country." She holds up a textbook. "And you can think about this as a collection of stories about ordinary people, just like all of us, who did ordinary things like get married and take trips, and maybe even train their pets." She points at Logan, who takes a bow from his desk. Everybody laughs again.

"But they also did extraordinary things that made our world what it is today. That's why the Living History Museum project is such an important part of the work you'll do this year. It's your chance to really experience the stories of some of the great individuals who have shaped our country, sometimes in big ways and sometimes in small. But all of them important."

Once again, all I can think is *Great*.

The sixth-grade Living History Museum is sort of like a pageant, a night when all the sixth graders, dressed in homemade costumes, have to stand around the auditorium, giving speeches as famous Americans from the past. Me and Sophia went last year to get ideas.

"I hope I get to be Sammy Lee," Sophia had said afterward. "The first Asian American to win a gold medal at the Olympics." She grabbed hold of my wrist. "Oh, Geez! Do you think there are any famous American *gardeners*? Because, if there are, that's who you should be."

Mrs. Ramos-McCaffrey takes a pile of bright pink papers off her desk. "March might seem like a long way off, but it will be here sooner than you think," she says, sending a stack of the papers down each row. "Take one and pass the rest down. This is some information for your parents—just the basics: dates, deadlines, expectations. That sort of thing. They'll hear more at Back to School Night."

I read the handout. It's filled with bullet points like blaring warning signs:

- Mark your calendars! This year's sixth-grade Living History Museum will be held March 3 at 5 p.m. You won't want to miss it.

Attention! Everyone is going to notice when Dad's not there.

- Students will be assigned a historical figure to study and impersonate. Grades will be based, in part, on the costume your child designs, so it's important to start planning right away.

Caution! Costumes cost money, and that's something we don't have right now.

- Students will have plenty of time in class to research and write their speeches, but they will need your help preparing to present them in front of a large audience.

Danger! Public speaking means talking. Like, in front of people.

"Please have a parent sign the bottom of the form and return it to me tomorrow," Mrs. Ramos-McCaffrey says. I fold mine in half and stick it inside my backpack.

"When do we get to pick names?" Taylor Lu asks.

"If we get through everything we need to cover today, maybe this afternoon."

Taylor squeals happily. I slouch lower in my chair and look down at my shoes.

⌒

When it's lunchtime, I stand near the end of the cafeteria line, not quite *in* the line, but also not quite out of it, so that everyone who comes in after me has to ask "Are you in line?"

Instead of actually deciding, I keep letting them go ahead of me. I should have gotten up earlier and made lunch at home. I didn't know it was going to feel like this, like everyone can *see.*

"No one is going to notice, you know."

"What?" I turn around. Logan is looking down at the blue-and-white-checked cafeteria tiles instead of at me.

"I mean…My mom said you guys…I mean, you're getting free lunch now, right?"

"Your mom's been talking about us?" My cheeks burn.

"No…Well, yeah. But not in a bad way. Don't be mad." He finally looks up.

I'm not mad. I am mortified. What else has she been saying?

"Anyway, you are, right? Getting free lunch, I mean?"

"It's only until…" Only until when? I don't know, so I swallow and nod.

"You never thought it was a big deal that I did, right?"

"Of course not." I had never even thought about it.

"Exactly." He steps in front of me and takes a tray off the top of the stack. "When you get up to the front, you hand them your student ID. No one else will even be paying attention. Not that it's any of their business, anyway. Come on."

I step in line behind Logan. I take a ham sand-
wich, an apple, a cup of chocolate pudding, and a
carton of milk. I carry my tray to the register but
can't bear to look up at the cashier. She holds out
her hand.

I hold my breath and give her my card.

"Thank you," she says, giving it back.

Logan waits for me near the register. "See?
That's it."

I smile. "That's it."

"They should just make it free for everyone,
you know?" Logan says, carrying his tray away to a
table at the other end of the cafeteria. "Then no one
would feel different."

I sit down across from him, but before I start
eating, I look around for a black ponytail and sun-
burnt nose. I didn't speak to Sophia all summer,
except when I lied and told her I had food poison-
ing that time she invited me to swim at her family's
club.

I'm listening so hard for her squeaky laugh
that I don't hear Logan at first when he asks me a
question.

"Huh?" I say, finally realizing he's talking to me.

He pops a grape into his mouth. "Never mind."

"No, what?"

He swallows and wipes his hand over his mouth. "I was just saying, do you remember how we used to play handball against my garage door all the time?"

"Hmm. I don't know. I guess I remember *beating* you at handball all the time."

"Like *one* time."

"Um, like *every* time."

"If it makes you feel better," he says, reaching over to pat my shoulder. "Anyway, I was just thinking, maybe we could play again if you want to come over sometime. And then maybe you can help me with Magdalena. If she ever comes back. I'm trying to fix up her aquarium. You know, so she'll actually want to stay there and stop sneaking out."

He stops, looks away, then adds, "You never come over anymore."

I open my mouth. I want to tell him that's not true. But it is. "Sure, I'll come over. I guess I can come over anytime. Now."

Both of us are quiet. Logan looks up as if he expects me to say something else. To talk about it. When I don't, he starts stirring his chocolate pudding.

I reach into my backpack, not searching for anything in particular, except for maybe a way to fill the awkward space between Logan and me. My fingers wrap around something I don't recognize at first. It's not a pencil—too thick. It feels like it could be a marker, but Mom and I didn't buy any.

I pull it out. Maribel's lip gloss. I must have knocked it into my bag with the school supplies this morning. I hold the tube between my thumb and index finger, tilting it one way and then the other, watching the glitter slowly swirl inside.

"What color?"

Kennedy Castro is leaning over my shoulder.

"What color?" she asks again. "It's Alma, right? From the Fairytale Collection?"

"Um, yeah. How'd you know?"

She doesn't answer, just rolls her eyes like it's obvious. "Can I see it?"

I give her the lip gloss, and she untwists the applicator wand. "My cousin has Poison Apple and Stroke of Midnight," Kennedy continues, swiping a shimmery smear of gloss across the back of her hand. "She never lets me borrow it."

She holds her hand up to the light. "But she doesn't have this one. It's pretty. Where'd you get it?"

I don't answer right away. Kennedy thinks the lip gloss is pretty. I wish the truth—that it's just a free sample I got for helping my sister talk a stranger into buying face cream that she probably didn't need and that *definitely* wasn't miraculous—weren't so boring. It's been months since I had something a little bit special, something someone else *wants*. Since I've felt someone wish they had what I have. And I don't want to let the feeling go.

And then I realize: Kennedy isn't letting go either.

Her grasp on the lip gloss only tightens when Ava Davis appears at her side and asks to try some on.

"I got it from my sister," I say, finally pulling the tube back. "She's an Alma..." I don't remember the title at first. "An Alma Glamour Associate. I *could* ask her to get you some, or maybe—"

An idea, small and fragile, is beginning to blossom. Kennedy and Ava lean in closer.

I look across the table at Logan. He has finished his pudding and is scraping the sides of the near-empty cup, pretending not to listen.

I think about Maribel, about what she would do. If she were here trying to sell a tube of lip gloss, it would seem as though she wasn't actually trying at all. Maribel would sound casual, cool, like she didn't care very much, one way or the other, whether the girls wanted to buy it. *No pressure or anything.*

"Or what?" Kennedy asks.

I clear my throat. "Well, it's just that I don't really like this color, anyway. And it does look really nice on...your hand. I guess...I could...I don't know, sell it to you?"

I wave the lip gloss like a wand. "I mean, if you like it. Or whatever." I start to put it away.

Kennedy's eyes widen. "Wait." She swings her backpack off her shoulder, unzips the front pocket, and frowns.

"All I have is four dollars. Is that enough?"

Ava nudges her shoulder in front of Kennedy's. "I have *five* dollars."

"Hey, she offered it to *me*."

I pluck four dollar bills out of Kennedy's fist and give her the lip gloss. Maybe this is just as easy as Maribel always makes it look. "Sorry, Ava. But don't worry. I bet I can get more."

As they walk away, Logan raises his hand for a high five. "Four dollars. Not bad. What're you gonna do with it?"

I know exactly what I'm going to do with it. Buy more lip gloss, and then sell that, too.

CHAPTER SIX

It takes as much energy to wish as it does
to plan.
—Eleanor Roosevelt

The Fresh New Face of Alma Cosmetics. Remembering the contest from Maribel's brochure, I write long division problems in the margins of my notebook paper to try to figure out how long it'll take me to get to five hundred if I sell five tubes of lip gloss a week. What about ten? Fifteen? Could I even sell fifteen in a week?

My hair is thick. Wavy like Dad's, and I almost always wear it tied back in a braid that falls halfway down my back—except for my bangs and the loose, flyaway strands that curl over my ears. I tug one of them and twirl it around my finger, trying to imagine my hair loose and flying out behind me as I ride in the front seat of a shiny silvery-purple convertible. *The Spirit of Success!*

I can just about picture it. Almost. But I can't hold on to the picture. I can't quite *believe* in it.

I look nothing like the girl in Maribel's catalog. But I try not to think about that. If I think about it, I'll never go through with my plan, and it's the best plan—the only one, really—I've had since we moved in with Nana.

Instead, I think about what Dad had said in our living room that afternoon last spring. "Game over."

Maybe if I win, I can show him it isn't. Maybe if I win, we'll finally stop losing things. I know five thousand dollars isn't enough to get our house back. But it might be enough to get Dad's truck fixed, or to repay some of the money he owes so he can come live with us again. It might be enough for that fresh start we've all been trying to find.

"Miss Zaragoza, are you still with us?"

"What? Huh?" I stop dividing when I hear my name.

Quiet snickers flutter across the desks.

"Sorry," I mumble.

"Come on up," Mrs. Ramos-McCaffrey says. "It's your turn to pick a name."

I walk to the front of the classroom. I feel everyone watching. Only this time, it doesn't bother me so much. This time, I let myself wonder if, just maybe, they're all staring at the fresh new face of Alma Cosmetics.

Mrs. Ramos-McCaffrey shakes an old coffee can filled with little slips of paper. "Go ahead."

I reach inside. Only a few names are left, and I stir them up with my fingers before choosing one. I pull it out and unfold it: *Lady Bird Johnson, 1912–2007, 36th First Lady of the United States.* "Oh!" I look up at Mrs. Ramos-McCaffrey.

She takes the paper and reads. "Ah. Well, some of these names might not be as familiar as others, at least not yet. But I think you just might find you have some things in common. If you'd like to draw again, though..."

I shake my head and take the paper back. "No, I want to keep it." My luck is already changing for the better.

When the last bell finally rings that afternoon, I walk out with Logan and see Grandpa's gold sedan waiting down the block, near where Maribel had dropped us off that morning.

"Want a ride home?"

"Nah, my mom said she'd pick me up at the library. I need to do some research on snake habitats—for Magdalena's aquarium, you know? And maybe I'll get a head start reading about Lafayette, hero of the American Revolution. See you tomorrow." He gives me a military-style salute, hikes up his backpack, and marches away.

"See you tomorrow."

I head for the Crown Victoria—until a tug on my backpack straps sends me stumbling backward.

"Geez! Found you!"

Back when we were in third grade, Sophia said I needed a new nickname. "Griselda is just...so... *you know*," she had said, wrinkling her nose.

I knew.

"And Geez isn't a name. It's what you say when

your dog chews up your best headband. So I've been thinking...what about *Zelda*?"

She had tried, I mean, *really tried*, but Zelda never caught on. Finally, even Sophia gave up and started calling me Geez, too.

Hearing her say it again after so many months makes me remember something I had read about Lady Bird Johnson once. How her real name—the name her parents gave her, I mean—was *Claudia*. Which is almost as beautiful as Maribel, to be honest. Lady Bird was just a nickname someone gave her when she was really little. A nickname that stuck for so long that hardly anyone called her anything else after a while. I wonder sometimes if she liked being called Lady Bird, or if she ever wished she could be Claudia again but finally just gave up trying.

Somehow, Sophia has always been Sophia. Never Sophie or Soph. Her name just fits that way.

She cut her hair short over the summer, to just past her chin. It's shiny black except for the ends, bleached reddish-brown from all the chlorine in the swimming pool. The last sunburn of summer is peeling off her nose. "I have to go. Mom and Lucas are already in the car, but I just had to see you. It's been forever. I'm so mad we're not in the same class this year, aren't you? Sorry I wasn't around for lunch. Mom pulled me out for an eye doctor appointment. Can you believe that? On the *first day*? I got to pick out new glasses, though."

Sophia and I have been friends since kindergarten, when her mom and my mom were room parents. They discovered our birthdays were a week apart, and we've celebrated together every year since.

Sophia's mom used to say that Sophia talked enough for the both of us. And it's true. Only, I decided after a while, Sophia and I sort of go together, anyway. We might not be exactly alike, but we match the same way the bright yellow-orange ribbon from Nana's gift-wrap stash balanced out the gentle blue of my shirt.

"I heard your class already picked names for Living History Museum?" she continues. "You guys are so lucky. We ran out of time. Who'd you get?"

"Lady Bird Johnson."

Sophia wrinkles her pink and peeling nose.

"You know. The one from my teacup? First Lady?"

"No, I know, but..." She puts her hand to her forehead to shade her eyes. "Over there. Isn't that your sister?

I turn around. Maribel is holding up a mirror for a woman who is making fish lips into it. Sugar Plum fish lips.

"Oh, yeah. My mom must have sent her to pick me up."

Sophia still looks confused.

"But shouldn't she be gone by now? I thought she was supposed to be—"

Of course. As far as Sophia knows, Maribel should have moved away to college over the summer. But there isn't time to explain it all.

"I better go," I interrupt. "See you at lunch tomorrow?"

"Yes!" Sophia's voice rises to a squeak. "Can't wait! Cute shoes, by the way. Oh!" She reaches down and picks a dandelion growing in the gap between grass and sidewalk. "Make a wish. Ready? One, two, three!" A flurry of cottony seeds floats between us before drifting away.

My wish hasn't changed since that afternoon last spring, when the sound of my heart thumping in my ears drummed away the sugary jingle of the ice-cream truck: that things go back to the way they were.

Only now, for the first time, I feel like there's something I can do to help that wish come true.

When I get to the Crown Victoria, Maribel is handing the woman a business card.

"That color really brings out your eyes, no kidding," she says. "Give me a call when you're ready to reorder." She sees me coming. "Geez, there you are. Let's get going."

Even before I buckle my seat belt, I pop open the glove box. I poke around but find only the owner's manual and old receipts from the mechanic: oil change, tune-up, new tires. Everything in order. I duck down and check under the seat. She must have another one in here somewhere.

"What are you looking for?"

"One of those Alma booklets, like you had yesterday."

"An Alma booklet?"

"Yeah, do you have one? I want to check something."

"You want to check something?"

I sit back up and slap my hand down on the seat. "Quit repeating everything I say. Do you have another one or not? Can I see it?"

"All right, all right. Geez, relax." Maribel tosses her makeup satchel onto my lap. "In there. Take as many as you want."

I pull my seat belt across my chest. Grandpa's car rumbles to a start as I riffle through Maribel's bag.

The booklets are held together inside a rubber band that looks as though it's about to snap. I pull one out and flip to the advertisement I had seen the day before.

The Spirit of Success! I read. *Are you between the ages of 12 and 19?*

Not quite, but I will be soon. I move on to the fine print.

If you're under 18, get a parent's permission and fill out the form below to become an Alma Cosmetics Junior Associate. Then, simply sell 500 tubes of Fairytale Collection lip gloss by December 31 to earn your spot in Alma's Fresh New Face Challenge!

A parent's permission. Considering one of

mine is hundreds of miles from here, and the other already hates the idea of her daughter selling makeup, getting a parent's permission might be an even bigger problem than my age.

"So, what, do you know someone who wants to sell makeup?" Maribel asks, tapping the steering wheel at a red light. "Tell them to call me. I get a bonus for every new associate I recruit."

"Maybe," I tell her.

I roll down my window and let the warm breeze ruffle my bangs and loosen my braid. I imagine five hundred tubes of lip gloss, lined up end to end. Five hundred glinting pinks and glossy reds and glimmering purples, all leading Dad back home, back to the way things used to be.

Maybe.

CHAPTER SEVEN

The independent girl is a person before whose
wrath only the most rash dare stand.
—Lou Hoover

Our city is almost completely flat. On a clear day,
you can look west toward San Francisco and see
the rolling Diablo Range that in the springtime
glows yellow with wild Spanish broom and golden
poppies.

But in summer, it's too hazy to see much farther than the gray freeway overpasses at the edge of
town. We're driving that way, past the mall where
we bought my shoes and the drive-through car-
wash where Maribel used to go once a week until

her car stopped really being hers anymore. We drive by two bus-stop benches with posters advertising Dad's old business, faded and peeling but still stuck there.

Before long, I'll look out my window and see a row of soaring cypress trees and then the proud and towering gates of the Valle del Sol Estates. Behind them are houses as huge, almost, as palaces, and Dad had made sure they had yards as green as parks. Maybe he hadn't dug all the holes or scattered all the fertilizer or installed all the sprinklers, but he had designed and organized and overseen so that everything went according to plan.

On the weekends, he used to take me to the worksite to see how houses became houses: from a flat concrete slab to a peaked-roof wooden skeleton in just a few weeks. He showed me landscaping sketches of streets lined with crepe myrtles, their magenta blossoms like tissue-paper flowers. He asked if I approved. When I told him it was missing azaleas and verbena and mountain lilac, he sketched those in, too.

Somehow, he even managed to get one of the streets inside Valle del Sol named after us. Zaragoza

Court. When the whole project was finished and houses were ready for people to buy, the four of us—Dad and Mom and Mari and me—had posed for a picture in front of one of the street signs, one of *our* street signs. I was sure we'd live behind those cypress trees someday, maybe even on that street.

All of it—the gates, the trees, the houses—are a blur across my window. And then they're behind us.

"Where are we going?" I finally ask. I hope she's going to sell more makeup. I never liked going with her before, but now, if my plan is going to work, I need to learn everything I can from Maribel.

"Tía Carla's," she says. "Mom wants me to bring you by so you can tell her all about your first day. She's working late over there again."

Tía Carla, Mom's sister, owns Belleza, a salon with two rows of black swivel chairs, each facing a gold-framed mirror that stretches from the gleaming wood floor to the chandeliered ceiling. If you stand in just the right spot, you can see a dozen different versions of yourself staring back out of the mirrors up and down the room. Tía Carla showed me once.

Mom started helping out at Belleza a few hours a week after Dad moved. And then a few hours a day. And lately, even longer. She sweeps the floors and answers phones and brings clients fizzy water with lime wedges while they wait for their appointments. I don't know if it counts as a job since Mom won't take money from Tía Carla, just tips from the clients. "I'm not going to let my baby sister bail us out," I heard her say, when Tía Carla tried to tuck a paycheck into Mom's purse.

So it's hard to know why she's at the salon all the time. I wonder if it's because she wants to forget we're living at Nana's house, which, trust me, is really hard to do while you're actually *at* Nana's house.

When Maribel and I walk into the salon, Mom is at the reception desk, pouring fresh water into a vase of irises. She puts down the pitcher.

"There's my sixth grader!" She gushes as though she were talking to a *first* grader. "I've been waiting for you!" A client whose hair is wound tightly in rollers glances over at me, smiles, and lifts her magazine back up to her face.

"How was your day? How were *both* your days?" Mom turns to Maribel with her round, hopeful eyes.

"Fine." Maribel's attention is already wandering to the far end of the salon where two clients sit under heat lamps. "Color processing?"

Mom sighs. "Just Señora Lopez. Mrs. King is waiting for her curls to set."

Maribel narrows her eyes. "Heat can cause just as much damage to the delicate hair shaft as harsh chemicals—without the right product."

"Maribel, please," Mom says. But it's too late. She's already headed over with her Alma catalog.

About this time last year, Maribel was busy applying to colleges all over the country. Most of her friends planned to attend schools nearby, but Maribel wanted to leave home. Her first choice was a college in Los Angeles. She wanted to study business. When she got in, she stuck her official acceptance letter to the refrigerator door and left it there for weeks.

But in the end, it was Dad who went to LA instead. He and Mom asked Maribel to postpone university for a year or two, to take classes at the community college in town until they could afford to help her with tuition again. She refused and started selling makeup with Alma. "I don't need anyone's help," she had said. "I'm going away to college. Even if I have to get there on my own."

Only, Mom is just as stubborn. She brought home registration forms from the community college and left them on Nana's kitchen table. Maribel wouldn't look at them, let alone fill them out. She and Mom finally stopped arguing about it when the registration deadline came and went. But worried lines still wrinkle Mom's forehead whenever she sees Maribel carrying her makeup bag. Like now.

"Refreshing as Rain, Alma's bestselling protectant spray, helps repair breakage and replenish moisture lost to heat styling," I hear my sister explain to the women under the heat lamps.

I want to go listen, too, but Mom isn't finished with me.

"So? How was it? Who's in your class? Did lunch go all right? I'm so sorry I wasn't there when you woke up this morning, but I knew Nana would take care of you."

"Well..." Inside my backpack is the pink flyer

Mrs. Ramos-McCaffrey gave us. I could take it out and give it to Mom. I could tell her not to worry. That I've figured out a way to pay for everything I need at school and maybe more. All she has to do is sign her name at the bottom of that Alma form.

But I saw the look she just gave Maribel. Of course she'll worry. I don't mention it.

"Logan's in my class," I tell her instead. "We gave him a ride this morning."

She brightens. "How is Logan? It seemed like the two of you were always missing each other this summer."

"He's good. Except for losing Magdalena again."

Mom shakes her head. "Better find her before Nana does. Come on, I want Tía Carla to trim your bangs."

"*Mom.*"

Most customers wait months to get an appointment with Tía Carla. I can walk in for a haircut whenever I want. Usually, I love sitting in her chair while she combs and cuts and whispers chismes about her other clients. But when Mom says she wants my bangs "trimmed," she means she wants them *hacked*—so short I really do look like a first grader until they grow out to a normal length again.

Mom has the same cherry-cola hair as Maribel, only hers falls just above her shoulders and never a millimeter longer. She was a reporter on TV before I was born. Once in a while, on weekend nights when Maribel was out and Dad was away, she and I would curl up on the couch and watch her old clips from Channel 4. "Good evening, I'm Sandra Zaragoza..." The way she strung them together, the big galloping syllables of her name sounded almost like magic words.

Mom stopped working when I was born, and she didn't go back. But she still looks camera-ready, and strangers in the grocery store still recognize her from television.

She still has a voice that makes you believe you can trust anything she says.

I follow her to a chair at the back of the salon and climb up. She whips a smock over me, pulls the rubber band off the end of my braid, and puts it in her pocket. She rests her chin on my shoulder, and our eyes meet in the mirror.

"I mean it. I'm really sorry I wasn't there this morning, corazón," she tells me again, but this time in a whisper. She kisses my cheek. "I should have been. I just thought—"

"It's okay," I interrupt. All of a sudden I feel as if I might start crying, and it's the last thing I want to do right here, wrapped in a leopard-print smock. I change the subject.

"Ms. Ramos got married this summer. She's Mrs. Ramos-McCaffrey now. She went to Spain. She showed us some pictures."

"Hmm," Mom said. She starts brushing my hair, smoothing out the crimps the braid has left behind. "Did you see Sophia? I bet she missed you at the pool this summer. I wish you would have gone when she invited you."

Not this again. I don't know how to explain to Mom why I'd been avoiding Sophia. I can hardly explain it to myself.

"I didn't see her until after school. She had a doctor's appointment. But we're gonna have lunch together tomorrow."

"Good!" She squeezes my shoulders. "And, Griselda! Why don't you ask her to come over after school?"

Tía Carla's reflection appears in the mirror before I have to think up an excuse.

In old pictures, from back when she was my age, Tía Carla has red-black hair like Mom's and Maribel's. But I have never seen it that color in person. And none of the shades I *have* seen ever last on Tía Carla's head for longer than a month. This time her hair is silvery blond with strands of pastel pink woven through. She pulls it back into a ponytail and nudges Mom out of the way.

"So, Griselda, are we going with purple highlights today, or blue?"

I smile.

"Just the bangs, Carlita." Mom is smiling, too, but her tone is warning. "And easy on the gossip."

"It's *networking*, Sandra." Tía Carla winks at me, then takes a pair of silver scissors out of a velvet-lined box. She spritzes my bangs and combs them straight down over my forehead. The ends tickle my nose, and, with my hands stuck under the smock, I squirm, trying to force back a sneeze.

"Sit still. How short are we going?"

"Just a little," I say.

"Griselda, I hate to see hair in your eyes," Mom says. "A good trim, Carla."

"But not *too* short," I add.

Tía Carla swivels me around so I'm facing her. Then she starts snipping, humming as she works. Little bits of hair land on my cheeks, as soft as snowflakes. Finally, Tía Carla spins me back around to look in the mirror. "How's that?"

"Actually, Carla, if you could take just a little more—"

But I am prepared this time. I hop out of the chair before Mom can finish. I unclip the smock, ball it up, and drop it in a laundry bin. "This is perfect. Thanks."

Tía Carla signals to an assistant to come sweep up the trimmings; then she and Mom follow me to the front of the salon, where Maribel is feverishly rearranging bottles. A stylist stands watching her with eyes wide and mouth half open.

"See, if you put the mousse for curly hair up here next to the shampoo and conditioner for curly hair, your customers will be more likely to buy all three." Maribel speaks as if she's in a race to get the words out. "They'll think they *need* all three to get results. Like, everything goes together. Get it?"

When she doesn't get an answer, Maribel looks up and asks again, *"Get it?"*

The stylist startles and begins shuffling hair products.

Satisfied, Maribel finally takes a breath. *"Then,"* she continues more gently, moving a basket full of lip balm and sample-size hair gel off a low shelf, "you should move all these little things up higher, put them over there by the register. It's easy to spend a few more dollars when your wallet's already open. And don't forget to leave out some testers. People love trying stuff on."

Tía Carla raises an eyebrow. "Someone's acting like she owns the place. Does this mean you're considering my offer?"

Tía Carla wants Maribel to go to cosmetology school if she's not going straight to college. She offered to pay the tuition and even give Maribel a job as an assistant stylist when she graduated. She says Maribel has what it takes to run Belleza someday.

"Still thinking about it, Tía."

Tía Carla is like an artist. To her, doing hair and makeup is like painting a picture or playing an instrument—like growing a garden was to me. It's not that way for Maribel, though. She might say she's still thinking about, but I can tell from her pressed-lip smile that Maribel isn't interested. She reminds me of the quote on the bottom of my Lou Hoover teacup. An independent girl.

"Well, whenever you're ready, you let me know." Tía Carla hugs us both goodbye, and Mom says she'll see us back at Nana's later, after she's helped clean up for the night.

CHAPTER EIGHT

Well-educated people can seek help for
themselves. They can help others.
—Laura Bush

The sky has turned pinkish orange by the time we
get back. Nana is dicing tomatoes at the kitchen
counter.

"You just missed your dad, mija. Why don't you
call him back? Dinner won't be ready for another
fifteen minutes or so."

I look at the phone. "I better start my homework
first. Then I'll call him."

But after homework, it's time to eat.

Later, I glance at the clock as I'm clearing the

dinner plates. I could call him now, but Mom will be back any minute, and I need to talk to Maribel without her hearing.

I find my sister in our room, sitting at the desk and lining up a row of Alma lip glosses. I close the door, stand next to her, and one by one, turn over the boxes to read the names of the colors: Waltz With Me, True Love's Kiss, Enchanted Castle.

"What are you doing? Leave those alone."

"Just looking. Can I have a few more of these?"

Maribel looks up at me and rolls her eyes. Then she goes back to her boxes.

"You're not even wearing the lip gloss I gave you yesterday. What do you want more for?"

I take a deep breath. "To sell it."

She stops, puts the boxes down, and looks up at me again. "To *what*?"

I pull the Fresh New Face entry form out from my back pocket and unfold it. I've filled in all the blank spaces—except for the one where a parent's or guardian's signature is supposed to go. "Sign this for me?"

She takes it and reads. "Five thousand dollars?" she mutters. She keeps reading, and I almost think she might go for it.

Then she hands the form right back. "Nuh-uh. No way. I'm not your parent."

"But you're an adult. That counts. They'll never know."

"And you're not twelve."

"But I will be by the deadline."

"Do you have any idea how freaked out Mom would be if she found out?"

"That's why we won't tell her. That's why I need *you* to sign it."

Maribel shakes her head. "You're at school all day. When, exactly, did you plan to sell"—she pauses and glances down—"five *hundred* tubes of lip gloss?"

I grab her elbow. "That's it. That's the point. I'm going to sell it at school."

I explain to her about Kennedy and how I sold my first lip gloss almost without even trying. How Ava would have bought one, too, if I had more. How if girls like Kennedy and Ava are wearing Alma lip gloss, everyone will want to buy some.

Maribel doesn't say anything. She just scrunches her eyes at me as if she's trying to see things clearly but can't quite pull it all into focus. So I keep talking.

"I'll split the profits with you, fifty-fifty. You'll make extra money without even trying."

That gets her attention. "How much did you say that girl paid for the lip gloss?"

"Four dollars."

Maribel groans. "Oh, Geez. Come *on*."

"What?"

"It's not enough." She drums her fingers on the desk, then pulls up the calculator on her phone and starts punching.

"The lip gloss retails for eight dollars," she says, but not exactly to me. "Alma associates buy everything at fifty percent off, so there's normally a four-dollar profit on each tube. We could drop the price to five or six dollars and still come out ahead. Seven would be better." *Tap, tap, tap.* "But that's probably too expensive for a bunch of schoolkids."

Maribel sets her phone down. "How much does lunch cost? If you pay with cash, I mean."

"Depends. Three or four dollars, I guess?"

"And how much does Mom give you?"

I look down at my shoes and don't answer.

"Geez, you know what I mean. How much did

Mom *used* to give you? Or, like, in general, how much money do kids usually get for lunch?"

"Mom always gave me five dollars, if I was buying that day."

"And I bet she never asked you for change back?"

"No," I admit. I always felt a little guilty about keeping Mom's money, but change from lunch was how I paid for teacups when I went to the thrift store with Nana, or packs of marigolds and snapdragons when Dad took me along to the nursery.

"So, say you saved the change every day. You'd have enough to spend six dollars a week on lip gloss, right?"

"Definitely."

Maribel starts stacking lip gloss boxes again. "Fine. I'll give you fifty cents a tube."

"No way, a dollar." Even if I don't win the contest, five hundred tubes of lip gloss means five hundred dollars; that's enough to buy a costume for the Living History Museum project, at least, and maybe even help Dad with the truck repairs.

"I'm taking all the risk."

"And I'm doing all the work." Arguing with Maribel is almost always hopeless, but I've made it this far, and I can tell she's at least a little interested.

She takes back the entry form. "Say I do this for you. It says here you also need to send in forty dollars for your starter kit of Fairytale Collection lip gloss. Do you even have forty dollars?"

"Not exactly, but..." I kneel down, reach under my bed, and pull out the box of teacups. "I have these. They're antiques. I thought if I sold some of them..."

The thing is, I don't know *which* ones yet. I hate to give up any of them. *But it's worth it*, I tell myself. *It's the only thing I can do to help us find our way back to normal.*

Maribel looks at the box and then quickly away again. Her mouth tightens. After a long pause, she says, "Better idea: I loan you the forty dollars, and all the profits are mine until it's paid off. Deal?"

My fingers twitch as I work out the math in the air. *Selling the lip gloss for six dollars each leaves a two-dollar profit. Forty dollars divided by two is...*

"Twenty tubes, and I've paid you back." I jump up and wrap my arms around Maribel's neck. "Deal!"

"Geez, relax." She lifts my arms off her neck and gives me her hand to shake instead. Then she counts out ten boxes of lip gloss. "Let's see how long it takes you to sell these."

I turn them over to check the colors. "Do you have any more Once Upon a Time? That's the one Ava wants—the same as Kennedy."

"Free piece of business advice: She'll want it even more if she can't have it. Trust me."

What choice do I have? I take the boxes and zip them inside my backpack, hoping Maribel is right.

The sky is inky dark behind Mom's old lavender curtains. The day is almost over, but in some ways it feels like a beginning. Full of possibility, like a first day is supposed to be. I fall asleep looking at my Lady Bird Johnson teacup, wondering what shade of lipstick she used to wear.

CHAPTER NINE

You have to have confidence in your ability,
and then be tough enough to follow through.
—ROSALYNN CARTER

The next day at lunch, just like she promised, Sophia finds me in the cafeteria line. I feel a tug on my backpack straps and stumble backward. "Guess who?" she says, and giggles.

Sophia has brought her lunch from home in a pink-and-blue-plaid bag with her initials stitched on top in gold.

"Logan's already out there, saving us seats. Why don't you go find him while I get my food?" I suggest. Even though Logan showed me that no one can tell the difference, I'm still worried Sophia will find out how I'm paying for my lunch—that she'll find out I'm *not* actually paying for it, I mean.

"That's okay. I'll keep you company."

"But the line's really long. Don't you want to start eating?"

"It's moving fast."

She probably won't even notice, I tell myself. *And so what if she does? She's my friend. I should just tell her anyway.* I put a slice of cheese pizza, a cup of diced peaches, a box of apple juice, and an oatmeal cookie on my tray.

We inch closer to the cashier. Sophia is describing the new glasses she picked out yesterday, but I'm having trouble paying attention to anything besides the bleeping noise the register makes as each student steps forward to pay.

Bleep.

"Thank you."

Bleep.

"Thank you."

We take another two steps closer. The sudden squeak of a sneaker against the tile floor startles me, and I almost drop my tray.

"Whoa, are you okay?" Sophia takes a step backward.

That's it. I drop back in line and return everything but the peaches.

"I'm not actually that hungry after all," I mumble. I still have the four dollars Kennedy paid me yesterday. I had wanted to save it, but I can spend a little on lunch.

"Seriously? That's all you're getting?" Sophia looks doubtfully at the cup of peaches. "I feel like I could eat ten of those."

"Big breakfast."

"Coach says never skip breakfast, but she *also* says never eat a heavy meal before getting in the pool, so now that we have practice at six a.m. every morning, I don't know *what* I'm supposed to do."

Sophia keeps talking as I pay the cashier then lead us to the table where Logan has already unpacked his brown paper lunch bag and is peeling wisps of mozzarella off a stick of string cheese. Just over his shoulder I spot Kennedy and Ava at the table behind ours. I reach around to pat the bottom of my backpack where ten tubes of lip gloss are stashed. I've made up my mind to sell three tubes before the school day ends.

That's it. Just three.

"I can do this," I murmur, too quietly for anyone else to hear. Kennedy and Ava are my best hope.

Sophia sits down and rips open the Velcro top of her lunch bag.

"Where's the rest of your food?" Logan asks when I sit down next to him with my peaches.

"Not hungry."

He shakes his head. "No one will notice," he says. "Or *care*."

I shoot him a pleading look, but fortunately, Sophia doesn't know what he means.

"He's right. You have to eat more than that." She takes a bag filled with almonds and dried cranberries out of her lunch sack. Next comes half a bagel smeared with peanut butter. Then a hard-boiled egg, a bunch of green grapes, and a plastic container full of bow-tie pasta noodles without any sauce. "Here. Take this."

She drops the bagel in front of me. I'm so relieved

and so hungry, I tear open the plastic wrapping and take an enormous bite. But the dough is so dense, and the peanut butter is so pasty, I can barely move my jaw enough to chew it.

Sophia studies my face as I struggle to swallow. "Sorry. You're gonna want something to wash that down. It's homemade, from this all-natural recipe book my mom's trying out. I probably should've warned you."

Logan slides his water bottle across the table. I gulp down half of it, then give the bagel back to Sophia.

I know I could have gotten my own lunch, and I know it isn't Sophia's fault that I didn't. But it doesn't seem fair somehow that she still has homemade peanut butter and a lunch bag with her initials embroidered on top. That she's acting as if nothing has changed. That for *her* nothing has.

I take one more sip of Logan's water to rinse away the bitter taste in my throat. "Thanks, anyway, Sophia. But I'm not that hungry. Really."

She tears off a piece of the bagel, pops it into her mouth, and chews. And chews, and chews, until she reaches for her own water bottle. "Whoa. Yeah, you'd have to be *real* hungry to choke that down. I wish my mom would let me buy lunch. You're so lucky." She takes the lid off her pasta, spears two bow-ties with her fork, then looks up at us. "So, did you hear they're trying to start up the chess club again? Are you gonna join? It's after school—I'll sign up if you do."

"How much does it cost?" Logan asks.

"I don't know."

"I'd rather go to the library after school. Do you wanna know what Lafayette sent George Washington as a present? *Dogs.* Seven of them, all the way from France."

Sophia slumps. "We still haven't picked names yet," she complains. "How about you, Geez—have you learned anything new about that Lady Bug person?"

"Hmm?" I'm trying to keep up with the conversation, but Kennedy and Ava look like they're almost finished eating, and I don't want to miss my chance. "Lady Bird, you mean?" I sit up higher on the bench and stretch my neck to try to see what Kennedy is doing. As she wads up her napkin, I pick up my backpack. "Be right back, you guys."

"Wait, where are you going?" Sophia says, putting down her pasta. "The student store's open during lunch. I thought we could go look before the bell rings."

I nod without looking back.

A step away from Kennedy's table, I stop. I square my shoulders the way I've seen Maribel do a million times. I breathe in through my nose, count to three, then breathe out through my mouth the way Mom is always saying I should to help settle my nerves. I step forward.

"Hi."

Kennedy and Ava don't notice me. Neither do any of their friends. I clear my throat, partly to get their attention and partly to cough out the wobble in my voice. No one looks up.

I'm about to turn around and go back to my table. I can try again after school, I decide. But then, in the very back of my mind, I hear Maribel. Her toe tapping on the cold bathroom tile. Her fist pounding on a closed door. *Oh, Geez.*

The fresh new face of Alma Cosmetics cannot just stand here shaking like a mouse.

I take another breath. "Um ... hey!" I say finally,

even louder than I mean to. The whole table stops talking.

Ava looks at me, then back at her friends, as if one of them might know why I'm standing there. When no one explains, she answers, "Uh, hey, Geez. What's up?"

"Hey," I repeat, not sure what to say next. I don't know what made me think this would be so easy. I should have practiced, or at least planned, what I was going to say. The whole table is still looking at me, and my cheeks feel as if they're turning as red as the lipstick in my backpack.

"So?"

"So. Um, I talked to my sister about that lip gloss you wanted?"

Am I asking her, or am I telling her?

Ava leans in closer to me. "Oh, yeah? Did you bring it?" Kennedy, who had started talking to the girl next to her again, stops and leans in, too.

I look from one to the other. "Uh...no. Unfortunately, Once Upon a Time is sold out right now."

"Oh." Ava starts to turn away. "Thanks, anyway."

"Wait!"

She looks up at me again. I unzip my backpack and pull out a handful of lip glosses.

"I don't have Once Upon a Time, but I do have these other colors."

Ava moves aside her lunch, and I arrange the makeup boxes on the table. "Here," I say, picking one out. "This would look great on you." It's called Poison Apple. I shake the tube out of the box and offer it to Ava.

It's a deep brownish-red, like an old brick fireplace. Ava looks at it for a long time. "I like it," she says after a while. "But it's too dark. My parents would never let me wear this."

Kennedy reaches for it. "Here, let me see."

I give Poison Apple to Kennedy and open another box for Ava. This time it's Glass Slipper: the palest pink, with a faint pearly shimmer.

"I bet they won't even notice you're wearing this one."

As Ava examines the tube of Glass Slipper lip gloss, Taylor and Hannah Sanchez reach over her, each grabbing one of the other boxes. I remember what Maribel said at Belleza, about customers loving to try things on.

"Um, you can go ahead and test it? If you want?" I suggest. "I mean, you should go ahead and test it. Do you want me to open them?"

Kennedy doesn't wait for my help. She twists off the top of her tube and swipes a layer of Poison Apple over her lips. "What do you think?" she asks Ava.

"Super dramatic."

"It's four dollars, right?" Kennedy asks me.

"Actually, it's six." I bite my lower lip. Maybe six is too high. "Yesterday was like a— a special."

She frowns, then shrugs. "Let me get my wallet."

Ava already has hers out.

"Can I borrow a dollar?" Taylor asks Hannah. "I'll pay you back tomorrow." Hannah pulls seven dollar bills out of a pouch in her binder. She hands one to Taylor and six to me in exchange for True Love's Kiss.

I can't help smiling as I walk back to my table with twenty-four dollars in my pocket and only six glosses left in my bag.

Logan is still there. One of his library books is open on the table, and he's showing Patrick Garcia a picture of a rattlesnake eating a squirrel.

"Where'd Sophia go?"

"Student store." Logan points.

Sophia is with Daisy Della Santo, a girl from her swim team, on the other side of the cafeteria where the student store is set up. Sophia tugs at the ends of her hair as if she's still not used to how short it is. A pink-and-orange friendship bracelet is knotted around her wrist. I hadn't noticed it earlier. We made dozens of them one weekend last winter when it was too rainy to go outside. Then we gave them to our classmates as valentines.

I rub my own wrist where I used to wear a matching one, but nothing's there. The bracelet isn't lost the way our house is—it's still mine—but it's gone just the same, misplaced somewhere with everything else I had to pack up and put away.

⁓

When school gets out that afternoon, I find Sophia in the hallway. I feel bad that we haven't exactly caught up, and that I sort of ditched her in the cafeteria, even if it was for a good reason.

"Find anything in the student store?"

"Got a couple of folders. And something for

you, too." She gives me a pencil, dark blue with the name of our school printed down the side in white letters.

"What for?"

"I just thought you'd like it. It changes color when you hold it. Try it."

I take the pencil and squeeze. Blue turns to green, then to red, under my warm fingertips. "Thanks," I say, wishing I had something to give her in return.

We walk outside together, but before we can get very far, two seventh graders step in our way.

"Ava said you're selling lip gloss?"

"Huh?" Sophia tilts her head and pushes her glasses up higher on her nose.

I take a step forward, almost in front of her. "Um, yeah. That's right."

We stare at each other for a few seconds.

"Well, do you have any more?"

I swing my backpack off my shoulder. "Oh! Yes, I do, actually."

Sophia whispers, "See you later," walking away as I fumble for the boxes.

Lifting my head to tell her goodbye, I notice

Grandpa's gold sedan pull over at the corner. I can hear the engine rumbling from across the street. Maribel leaves it running as she holds an arm out the window and waves me over. I wave back, then turn to the seventh graders.

"There's only a few left," I tell them, holding two of the last boxes in my fist. "This one is Waltz With Me, and this one is Fairest in the Land."

They snatch away the boxes hungrily.

Honk. Honk.

It's coming from Grandpa's car. Maribel is waving again. I point at the girls. "Just a minute," I call out.

"Geez!" she yells back out the window.

I reach into my bag again to fish out another box.

"And this one is called Enchanted Castle. It's really sparkly?"

The horn blares again. This time when I look over, Maribel is standing outside the car with her hands on her hips. She reaches inside the window.

Honk. Honk. Honk.

"Okay, okay, I heard you." I take all the makeup back.

"Hey!"

"Sorry. That's my ride. But I'll bring them back tomorrow, okay?"

"But wait, I have the money right here."

Honk.

"Sorry," I say again, already walk-jogging away. "Tomorrow."

"Don't forget—save Enchanted Castle for me!" one of the girls shouts after me.

Maribel's scowl matches mine when I get to the car.

"Geez, didn't you see me? Or hear me?" she demands, turning the key as I hop into the front seat. "I have an appointment with a client. You're going to make me late."

"I was about to make a sale," I argue. "Maybe two."

She waves off my complaint as though shooing a mosquito away from her face. "They'll be first in line tomorrow. Just watch."

CHAPTER TEN

The habits of a vigorous mind are formed in
contending with difficulties.
—Abigail Adams

Maribel was right.

Of course.

Beth Murphy, one of the seventh graders from yesterday, is waiting for me when I get to school the next morning. "You remembered to bring the lip gloss, right? Enchanted Castle?" She holds out six dollars.

"I have it right here." I let her follow me into the building and down the hall. "But there's another color you might like, too."

Last night, Maribel replaced the four glosses I sold during lunch with four new ones, all in Sugar Plum. For each one of them I sell, she's promised me an extra fifty cents off the forty dollars I owe her. The more items of the month on her sales sheet, the bigger her bonus. And as far as I'm concerned, an extra fifty cents is another step closer to bringing Dad home.

Beth and I stop outside my classroom. I dig into my backpack for a tube of Sugar Plum lip gloss and offer it to her.

"It's really...purple," she says doubtfully.

"Well," I scramble, trying to remember the lines I had practiced in the bathroom mirror last night. "It...it looks better when it's on. You should try it. Here, I have a mirror." Maribel had sent me to school with one of those, too.

I flip open the mirror and give the lip gloss to Beth. I take the top off for her to make it even easier to try on.

She applies a thin layer and presses her lips together.

"See? So...*plummy*," I say, trying to sound encouraging. Beth doesn't seem convinced, though.

"Mmmm."

She smiles into the mirror. Then pouts. "Can I see Enchanted Castle again?"

"Sure. Let me find it."

I try not to sound too disappointed. At least I tried. At least she still wants to buy *something*. But when I find Enchanted Castle in my backpack and hand it over to Beth, she doesn't trade in Sugar Plum. Instead, she holds on to both lip glosses, a tube in each hand, as though she's weighing one against the other.

"Dad *did* give me a little extra money this week," she says to herself. "It was supposed to be for pens and stuff at the student store, buuuut..." She slips both glosses into her jeans pockets. "I'll take both."

"Both? Are you—"

I'm about to ask if she's sure. Maybe she really needs those pens. But then I think, she probably has plenty of pens already. And anyway, it's not really any of my business how she spends her money.

"I mean, are you going to wear Sugar Plum to class?" I ask instead. "Or do you want to wipe it off and wear Enchanted Castle? I have a pack of tissues if you need one."

⌒

Mrs. Ramos-McCaffrey takes us to the library to research our Living History Museum projects. I find a portrait of Lady Bird Johnson wearing a yellow dress like the one on my teacup, only in this picture she's standing next to a man in a tuxedo. He has bushy eyebrows and a joking smirk, and looks like he could be anyone's grandpa. The kind whose ears are a little too big, and who knows a couple of magic tricks and a bunch of terrible knock-knock jokes.

While that man was president, Lady Bird traveled the country, planting wildflowers along the roadsides and in dreary city parks where children couldn't play anymore. She fought for a law to make the highways more beautiful, even though people made fun of her for it.

As much as I love flowers, though, and as much as they make me remember gardening with Dad, I'm more interested in something else I find out about Lady Bird Johnson: She had a business, too. After her mom died, Lady Bird bought a radio station, one that owed so much money it was about to shut down. Just like Dad's business.

But somehow she saved it. Somehow she turned that radio station into a company that turned *her* into a millionaire. Nothing I read explains exactly how she did it, though. And that's the part I really need to know. I wish there were some way to ask her.

◡◞

By Friday afternoon, I've sold twelve tubes of lip gloss, including all four of the Sugar Plums. Six girls have already told me they want to buy some on Monday, after their parents give them their allowances over the weekend. I might be able to pay back my sister sooner than I'd thought.

Still, twelve isn't even close to five hundred. I'm going to have to work fast if I want to qualify for the Fresh New Face contest. Four-lip-glosses-a-day fast. Even on weekends. The longer I think about it, the more I wonder whether it's even possible.

When I get home from school, I go to the bedroom to put my backpack away for the weekend.

Maribel is at her desk, counting and calculating.

"Here." I give her my week's earnings.

"Good timing," she says. "Your starter kit came today." She points to my bed. A small purple box rests on top of my rumpled blanket.

Maribel adds up dollars and quarters while I flop onto my bed with a pair of scissors to open the Alma box.

"Twenty-four dollars, plus two more for selling the item of the month," she announces after counting twice. "Pretty good for your first week."

"But not good enough."

And then I think, maybe I can't ask Lady Bird Johnson for business advice. But there's always Maribel.

"Hey, Mari?"

"Hey, what?"

I turn over the box. Packing peanuts and lip gloss boxes tumble onto my bed. "Well, what if you wanted to sell four or five of these every day?"

"Geez, I sell, like, eleven or twelve of those every day."

"But if you were me, I mean. How would you do it?"

"If I were you?" She gets up from the desk and sits on my bed so the makeup pile is between us. With her back against the wall and her bare feet hanging off the edge of the mattress, she looks like my sister again, not the slick, all-business sales-woman she has become over the past few months.

She picks up one of the boxes and studies it. "What would you say was the most popular color this week?"

"Everyone asked for Once Upon a Time, but you only gave me that one, and there aren't any in this box. Maybe when I order again next time, I can ask for extra—"

"No, that's good," she interrupts. "You need some exclusive shades. 'Get it now or lose it for-ever.'" Those, she explains, will get the attention of customers like Kennedy, people who like having things that other people can't have and who, most of all, like to stand out.

"Do you have an extra notebook? Start keeping track of the other popular colors and make sure you always have a lot of them." Those, Maribel says, aren't for people who want to stand out, but who want to feel as if they belong.

116

I take my black-and-white composition book out of my backpack and write *Glass Slipper* inside the back cover.

‿⁓

At first I mistake the splashing sound that wakes me up the next morning for the birdbath in our old backyard. But after I rub my eyes and clear my head, I realize it must be Nana, filling a bucket with water to scrub Grandpa's Crown Victoria. I'm up, anyway, and since Maribel and I have been borrowing it so often lately, I feel as though I should help her. I change into a tank top and shorts and walk outside in flip-flops.

When Nana sees me, she points at a bucket at the edge of the driveway. She's wearing her chanclas—a pair of old bath slippers—a checkered shirt, and faded black sweatpants, cut off just below her knees.

On the ground next to the bucket, Nana has left a pile of rags made from old T-shirts and bleach-spattered towels. I pick one up, dunk it in the sudsy water, wring it out, and carry it, dripping, to the passenger side of Grandpa's car.

Nana doesn't say anything, and I like the quiet. The only sounds are the *splash* and *swab*, *splash* and *swab* of our rags, and the twittering of finches in her apple tree—one more thing that grew where no one expected it to. The fruit is small and bitter, though. Only the birds will eat it.

After we're finished washing, I hose away the soap while Nana goes back inside for some fresh towels. By now the sun is bright enough to help us along, and we finish drying the car in only a few minutes. Satisfied, Nana dumps the bucket over the lawn and gathers up the rags.

"I'll be right in. I'm just going to pull some of these weeds...from the toilets."

Nana chuckles. "Ándale."

The weeding doesn't take long. Before I go back inside, I pull up some of the mint, too. It's just going to grow back, of course. I know it will. But I'm sick of seeing it spread and not doing anything about it.

"Bring me some of the mint leaves, mija," Nana calls out the window. "I'll put it in some iced tea. They say it's going to be another hot one today."

Mom is on the phone, alone in the kitchen,

when I get back with the mint. She's rubbing her temple with one hand while the other one clutches a letter so tightly, she's crumpling its edges.

I fill a glass with water, stick the mint inside, and leave it on the windowsill above Nana's sink.

"I see," Mom says. "Well, thank you for your time." I turn around when I hear the phone thud against the table.

Mom squeezes her eyes shut. When she opens them and sees me, she blinks again, and the lines between her eyebrows soften.

"You got an early start," she says. "Nice of you to help your nana."

"Dad coming?" He usually gets to Nana's house before breakfast when he visits on weekends. He likes to drive early, when the roads are still clear.

Mom gives me a sad half-smile, one I recognize from her old news tapes. It is a smile that promises the bad news she's about to deliver isn't actually as bad as it might sound. Trust her.

She breathes in through her nose—*one, two, three,* I count in my head—and out through her mouth. "He really *wanted* to visit," she says. "He misses you. *So* much. But he has a project coming up, and he needed to stay and get ready. It's only a small job, but who knows? Maybe it'll lead to something bigger. Wouldn't that be great? Just what we need right now."

We both glance down at the paper Mom's still holding. She slides it under Nana's fruit bowl.

Dad used to drive up to see us every weekend, back when we first moved in with Nana. It didn't last very long, though. Pretty soon, two weeks would slip by between visits. Then three. I try to remember the last time he was here. It's been about a month, I think. I would have been more surprised if he had actually shown up this morning.

"You're not too disappointed?"

I shake my head. I feel worse about Mom having to tell me than about my having to hear it.

She gets up and musses my bangs. "Good. I'm going to go shower. Why don't you give Sophia a call, see if she's free to come over?"

"Yeah, maybe."

I sit down at the table and take a banana out of the fruit bowl. When I hear the bathroom door click shut and the shower water start to run, I pull out the letter she left behind.

It's from the mechanic, about Dad's truck.

PAST DUE, it reads at the top.

Vehicle will be repossessed and sold if balance is not paid within 90 days.

CHAPTER ELEVEN

What day is so dark that there is no ray of
sunshine to penetrate the gloom.
—MARY TODD LINCOLN

I didn't realize they could just sell his truck like that.
There's no fresh start without Dad's truck. Even if
I wanted to, I can't invite Sophia over today. I need
to sell lip gloss. Four tubes a day, I remind myself.
Even on weekends. I need ideas. I need help.

I need Maribel.

She's in our bedroom, frowning at eye-shadow
palettes and moisturizer jars and perfume bottles
as if they are pieces in a puzzle she's trying to put

together. Already stacked next to her makeup bag are fifteen boxes of Sugar Plum lip gloss.

She's so focused on packing up makeup that she doesn't hear me come in and jumps when I clear my throat.

"Geez!"

"Sorry."

"Don't sneak up on me like that."

"Dad's not coming after all."

"Shocker." She rummages through containers of blush, in every shade from strawberry lemonade to fruit punch.

I pick one up. Gorgeous as Guava. "So, can I go with you today?"

"Put that back." She swats at my hand. "What? No. Sorry, Geez."

"Come on. Why not?"

"Listen, I know you're all sad and lonely and confused about everything, but not this time. This is business." She hasn't done her hair yet. It's loose and wavy, and when it falls into her face, she twists it into a bun that she holds in place with her pencil.

"But I go door-to-door with you *all the time*."

"Geez, I'm not going door-to-door today. I'm going to Ms. Dominguez's."

"Tía Carla's friend? With *all* of this?" Ms. Dominguez wears a lot of makeup, but still. Maribel has already packed enough to last her years, and she keeps adding to the pile: brow pencils, bronzers, nail polish.

"She invited some of her friends over for a party," Maribel explains. "I'm going to make them over, show them some samples, and you know"— she squeezes an eyelash curler open and shut before tossing it into her bag—"get them to buy it."

The women in Ms. Dominguez's living room can't be so different from the students in the El Dorado School cafeteria. I could learn so much just from watching Maribel. "But I don't understand why I can't go with you."

"This could be a really important new market for me, and it's all about word of mouth. I have to make a good impression. Another time, okay?"

It feels like a door shutting in my face. But if there's one thing I've already learned from my sister, it's never to give up before you find another way in. I start building a tower, stacking mascara boxes one on top of another.

"How did you get so good at business, anyway?" I try to sound casual, not daring to look Maribel in the eyes. "Did you take classes for it? Like, in high school or something?"

She pulls a mascara off the top, and the whole tower tumbles. I help her reorganize the boxes and pack them into her satchel. "Classes? No. I don't know. I guess I'm just good at figuring out what people want."

"You mean it comes *naturally*? I bet I could learn a lot from you."

She lays her hands on my shoulders. We're almost nose-to-nose, and I can't help but look her in the eyes. "Geez, I know what you're doing, and I already told you. Another time."

But I don't have time to wait. "I could help you. I can write down the orders and open up boxes so you have more time with the customers."

She doesn't say anything, just gets back to work. I consider it progress.

"Plus, the more I learn from you, the more

I'll sell. And the more I sell, the more money *you* make."

She stops and turns around to face me. "What I don't understand is why you're even doing this.... You know what? Never mind. I don't want to know. Fine. If it means you'll quit nagging me, you can come. As my assistant. My *silent* assistant."

"Thank you!"

"As long as you do everything I say and stay out of the way."

"Promise." I hurry to the bathroom down the hall to shower and change while Maribel finishes packing.

~

Carolina Dominguez, one of Tía Carla's clients from when she was just starting out, from long before she became a hairstylist to the rich and glamorous, lives somewhere inside Valle del Sol. When Maribel stops at the security gate, a guard walks out of the shed and up to her window. She rolls it down and smiles. "Good morning. We're here with Alma Cosmetics to see Carolina Dominguez."

The guard nods. "Name?"

"Maribel Zaragoza."

He looks over at me.

"And Griselda Zaragoza." He writes down our names and gives Maribel a parking permit to hang from her rearview mirror. The mechanical gate lurches open, and the guard waves us through.

"Wait!" Maribel calls, after he's turned around to go back inside his shed.

"Is there something else I can assist you with, miss?"

She unzips her bag and reaches inside. "I hope you don't mind my saying so, but I couldn't help but notice that your cuticles are looking a little dry."

He holds his hand up in front of his face, then buries it in his pocket.

"It's really no wonder. You must be in and out of the sun all day. I just want to leave you with this sample of Light as Feathers hand cream by Alma Cosmetics. It's dye-free and scent-free—you won't even notice you're wearing it. But, I promise"—she holds a hand to her heart—"your nails will know the difference."

The guard's hand is still in his pocket. He doesn't move.

Maribel shakes the sample-size bottle at him. "Here you go."

Finally, he takes it.

"Enjoy! And, while we're here, let me give you my card in case you decide to place an order."

We've been sitting outside the gate so long it has swung shut again. The guard reopens it and we drive into the Valle del Sol Estates.

The streets here are narrower than outside, and lined with pink and white crepe myrtles, Dad's old sketches come to life. We roll by a lush, green park. There's a pond in the middle where ducks are swimming, and all around it, cedar benches and shade trees.

That day Dad had brought us to see our street sign, the houses were newly finished, just about ready to be sold. Next to them, the trees and flowers looked scrawny and scraggy and much too small.

"This is *it*? This is all you're planting?" I had asked. Maribel elbowed me in the ribs, but I couldn't help it. I knew we were supposed to be proud of his work, but it looked as if Dad had messed up, miscalculated somehow.

He laughed and tickled me under my arms.

"Come back after a few years and then you'll see, mijita. Landscapes take time to grow into themselves. Just like you."

Later, he led us on a tour through one of the houses. I used to wonder what it would be like to live inside a dollhouse, and right then I knew, it would be exactly like that: everything spotless and untouched and plastic-smelling.

He was right about the landscaping, I think, as Maribel parks. Everything has grown exactly as he trusted it would. It's as if the plants I had seen before were the first reedy notes of a song in his head, and now they've turned into a symphony. It makes me wonder: If Dad had been able to make sure an entire *neighborhood's* worth of gardens would keep growing, years after he planted them, why couldn't he hang on to the one that mattered most—ours?

Maribel pulls down the sun visor to check her lipstick and eye shadow in the mirror, then unlocks the doors.

"Remember," she says, "my assistant."

"Your assistant."

"And you'll do everything I say."

"I *know*, Maribel."

We get out and walk up the long driveway to Ms. Dominguez's house.

On either side of the stone walkway leading up to the door are gardenia bushes. The leaves, which should be a dark, glossy green, are sickly and yellow. These plants need fertilizer, maybe. Or more water. It could be anything with a gardenia. It's a plant that's as finicky as its creamy white blossoms are beautiful. Gardenias like to be warm, but not hot. Damp, but not wet. They're too much trouble, even for me—and it looks like for Ms. Dominguez, too.

Maribel knocks on the door. She's wearing a black dress under her purple Alma blazer, and if she's even a little nervous about her first makeover party, I can't tell. She stands with her shoulders back, looking straight ahead, her face blank until Ms. Dominguez opens the door.

Then Maribel beams.

"Greetings from Alma, the Soul of Beauty."

Ms. Dominguez throws her arms around Maribel's shoulders and kisses her cheeks, leaving behind bright pink lip prints on both sides. "Mija, you look so grown-up!" She sees me. "And you brought Geez along, too?"

For a flicker of a moment, Maribel looks nervous. She opens her mouth to explain, but Ms. Dominguez isn't finished yet. "Maribel, you think of everything. Geez can watch the little ones while you make the rest of us beautiful." She tosses her coppery hair.

Gold bangles jangle on Ms. Dominguez's wrist as she takes my hand and leads me into the house. "Let's fix you a plate—you like chilaquiles, don't you?—and then maybe you can keep Izzy and Gonzalo busy in the playroom while your sister shows us some makeup."

I look over my shoulder at Maribel, my eyes begging her to say something so I don't get stuck babysitting. I'm here to watch her, not them.

She wipes off Ms. Dominguez's kisses with a Kleenex and shakes her head—just barely, but enough for me to know not to argue.

In the playroom, Izzy and Gonzalo, the three-year-old Dominguez twins, have built a tower of wooden blocks almost as tall as they are. Izzy flings a stuffed bunny at it, and the blocks clatter to the floor. Gonzalo cackles. "Again, Iz, do it again."

I kneel on the carpet to help them stack. A little while later, the doorbell rings, and I hear Ms. Dominguez welcome another guest.

"Good news. Maribel brought her sister along to keep an eye on the little ones while we mamis enjoy ourselves. Just drop Vito off in the playroom with Griselda and come pour yourself a glass!"

For the rest of the morning, I button up doll clothes and pretend to lick Play-Doh ice-cream cones, as the sounds of Maribel's party drift down the hall: Sometimes there are cheers, and sometimes *ahh*s of admiration. But mostly what I hear is laughter. Once, when I bring Izzy out for a glass of water, I peek into the living room where Maribel has arranged makeup and lotion, powders and perfumes around two table-top mirrors. She massages a dollop of moisturizer into a woman's hand, then holds it up to show the others.

"You can see the difference already."

They nod eagerly, and Maribel passes around samples.

⤴

It's almost lunchtime when Ms. Dominguez, bracelets still jangling, returns to the playroom. Since the last time she checked in, her nails have been painted red, and her eyelids have been outlined in metallic blue. Her cheeks are bright pink, but I can't tell whether that's from Maribel's blush or all the laughing.

"Mija, you were wonderful. How smart of Maribel to bring you along. She's just finishing up. You go help her. I can take over in here."

Some of the guests linger in the living room, flipping through catalogs and checking out the makeup that's still left on the display tables—just a few tubes of lipstick, some mascaras, and perfume. Everything else has been sold. Maribel is standing in the entryway, saying goodbye to a line of women, each of them carrying a lavender Alma shopping bag.

"That eye cream should last you at least six weeks—only use a dab at a time," Maribel tells one of them before slipping a business card into her purse. "That's my number. Give me a call when you're ready to reorder."

She steps over to the next woman. "You look amazing. Here's my card. You let me know if you ever need me to show you how to do that smoky eye again."

After all the guests have gone home and Maribel has repacked her bags, Ms. Dominguez walks us to the door. As I'm stepping outside, back onto the stone walkway, she taps me on the shoulder, then presses something into my palm. "A little something for all your help this morning."

I don't unfold it until we're back in the car. A twenty-dollar bill. Maybe getting stuck on babysitting duty wasn't so bad after all. After adding in my earnings from last week, I have more than enough to pay back Maribel.

"Here," I say, dropping the bill into the cup holder while Maribel takes off her blazer. "Now you owe *me*."

She folds the money into her wallet and sits down. "Better idea: You give this to me and consider it an investment in some new product."

"New product?"

"Sure. More makeup. Different kinds. A person only needs so much lip gloss."

"But I need to sell five hundred tubes of *lip gloss*."

"For that contest? Fine, so you keep selling lip

gloss. But what if you meet a customer who doesn't want lip gloss, she wants eye shadow? If you have eye shadow to sell her, you keep her happy *and* you make a couple more bucks."

"*You* make a couple more bucks, you mean."

"Are you here for business advice, or what?"

"Fine. Keep the twenty dollars. Reinvest it."

"Good." She drops an Alma catalog and a stub of red lip pencil onto my lap. "Circle anything you can sell for six dollars or less. That's what you'll order."

So as Maribel drives back through Valle del Sol, back through the gates, and back to Nana's house, I comb through the catalog, page by page. I draw thick red circles around anything you can buy with a week's worth of saved-up spare change: silver eyeshadow called Starlit Walk, blue eyeliner called Wishing Well, and emerald nail polish called Deep Dark Woods.

The back sides of seed packets have directions written on them in tiny letters. They tell you when to plant the seeds, how far apart to place them. They explain how much water each plant needs and how much sunlight. The Alma catalog doesn't come with instructions like that. But I study it the same way I used to study my seed packets, trying to learn everything I can to help my plan take root and grow.

CHAPTER TWELVE

Life does not seem very simple just now, but
kind thoughts like yours help to make it so
in time.
—EDITH ROOSEVELT

I cut fifty strips out of Nana's old wrapping paper,
bend them into links, and tape up the long chain
inside my half of the closet. For every ten tubes of
lip gloss I sell, I snip off a link.

By the time November comes, the chain is only
fifteen links long. Just like we had agreed, half of
my profits keep going to Maribel. I spend some
of what's left over on lunch and snacks and school
stuff—like that time we needed money for a field

trip to the museum, or when there was a lab fee for science class, and I didn't want to bother Mom with it. I invest a little in extra makeup. But most of the money gets hidden away under my bed, in the box with the teacups.

I've learned that Monday, after parents have handed out allowances for the week, is the best day to make sales. Money earned dusting coffee tables, weeding yards, walking dogs, and drying dishes can be exchanged for shimmery, sparkly, shiny lip gloss. So every Monday I make sure to bring new shades.

Once, after school, I overhear an eighth grader talking with a friend about her birthday party. It has to be perfect, she says, different from anyone else's. It has to be what everyone talks about the next week at school.

I walk right by them at first, but then I think about Maribel and the guard at Valle del Sol. Maribel wouldn't walk past an opportunity like this one. I turn around.

"Were you just talking about your birthday party?"

They exchange an irritated glance.

"Sorry. Eighth graders only."

"Right. I get it. But I was just thinking, you know what would make a perfect party favor? Something no one else would have? Something everyone would talk about?"

They look at each other again, less annoyed this time but still skeptical.

"Why? Do *you* have something?"

"Maybe." I reach into my backpack. "It's called Cast a Spell," I say, pulling out the lip gloss. "It's a special-edition shade. It just came in yesterday, and I hear it's already on backorder."

One of the girls takes the tube from me. "What's so special about it?"

"It changes color with your mood, from pale pink to deep red." I take the lip gloss back. "But if you're not interested..." I start to walk away.

"No wait," the girl says, chasing after me. "I'll take them. Just promise you won't sell this color to anyone else."

For eight dollars a tube, two dollars more than my usual price, I promise.

Another time, a girl in my class, gives me two dollars a week, sometimes counting it out in nickels and dimes, until she's paid for a tube of Romantic as Rose, a dusty pink. I can tell no one has just given her the money, that she's had to save it. Coin by coin, like the paper chain in my closet. For free, I throw in an eye shadow Maribel had given me after one of her customers returned it, opened but unused. It was called Cobblestone, a bluish silver. "You'll be the only one at school who has it," I tell her.

But my best customers are still Kennedy and Ava and their friends, especially after I start bringing them copies of Maribel's Alma catalogs. They're willing to pay in advance if it means they get to order the newest colors ahead of anyone else. Before long, I'm spending most of every lunch period at their table, watching them circle their favorites. I know they're not really my friends; I'm only sitting there to sell makeup. But I like it that way. They don't care that I'm living at Nana's house, that Dad lost his business, or that Mom can't afford all the things their mothers keep buying them. They don't know. They would never even think to ask.

Sometimes Logan sits with us. He sniffs the scented lip glosses and lets the other girls test new polishes on his fingernails. But other times, he sits back at our old table, working on designs for the new shelter he's building—out of some Alma boxes I gave him—to put inside Magdalena's terrarium. "I keep finding her inside Mom's shoes. I think she just wants a place to hide."

Logan is a little like a daylily, I decide. Blooming anywhere, without any fuss. Sophia is a zinnia, cheerful and sun-loving.

I'm not sure what kind of plant I'd be. Mom seems to think I'm like one of Ms. Dominguez's gardenias, something fragile that might shrink and wilt if the sun doesn't shine just right. That must have been the reason my parents told Maribel but not me that Dad's business was in trouble. That Mom still hasn't mentioned Dad's truck. That she keeps insisting everything is going to be fine.

But, slowly, I'm beginning to feel more like Lady Bird Johnson's wildflowers: sturdier than I look, growing even where you'd least expect.

$$\sim$$

It's Thursday, and I'm sitting at the end of Kennedy's lunch table, holding up a mirror while Taylor tries on Twinkling Tiara. Someone tugs on my braid. Expecting another lip gloss customer, I whip around and flash my brightest Maribel smile. "I'll be right with you, just one sec.... Oh."

It's Sophia.

She takes a step backward. "Sorry. I didn't mean to bother you."

Sophia and I tried having lunch together a few more times at the beginning of the school year, but I've been so distracted with selling makeup that after a while she started sitting with Daisy instead.

"No, that's okay. We were just finishing up."

Taylor gives me six dollars for Twinkling Tiara. I fold it into my wallet and swing my legs off the bench. The rest of the girls go on talking behind me.

"What's going on? You don't want to buy any of this stuff, do you?"

Sophia wrinkles her nose. "Makeup? No. It's just that my birthday—our birthdays, I mean—they're coming up?"

"Right." I force myself to nod. It's not that I'd forgotten, just that I haven't spent much time thinking about it. *Any* time, really.

"And," she continues, the corners of her lips

beginning to curl into a smile, "my mom says she'll take us to the mall on Saturday—you know, to celebrate? We can go shopping, have lunch in the food court. Sort of on our own. Mom'll be there, but not, like, *with* us, with us. So, can you come?" She's bouncing on the balls of her feet now.

I don't want to let Sophia down, especially since it's my fault we hardly talk anymore. But Maribel and I have a makeover party scheduled for Saturday. She's been bringing me along ever since that first one at Ms. Dominguez's house. Her clients spend more if they don't have to worry about watching their kids—and I always leave with a tip for babysitting. I can't give up the money, not with the bill for Dad's truck still unpaid.

"That sounds fun." It's not really an answer, and Sophia doesn't let me get away with it.

"*Pleeease?* Come on, Geez. We *always* celebrate our birthdays together, and we haven't hung out in *forever.*"

Something about the way she says *always* makes it impossible to say no. I know what that feels like, when things aren't the way they always were. "Okay. I'll ask my mom."

But I don't have to ask. I already know what Mom's going to say: *Griselda, that's a* wonderful *idea.*

⌒⌒

"Griselda, that's a *wonderful* idea," she says when I mention it at dinner. "You two girls used to be inseparable, and now you hardly see each other. It'll be good for you to get out of the house, spend some time with someone your own age."

Spend some time away from Maribel, she means.

Mom has never said I can't tag along with Maribel when she's selling makeup, but since I still haven't told her about the Fresh New Face contest, she can't figure out why I'd want to. "Isn't it boring for you?" she asked when we got back from a make-over party last weekend. "Your sister isn't putting you up to this, is she?"

Once in a while, when we're home alone together, she tries to pry information from me. "Is your sister dating someone or something?"

"*Mom.*"

"Well, what is she doing with all her money?

She doesn't have new clothes. She doesn't go out anymore, unless it's to see a client."

"I don't know. There's this car. . . ."

"A car?"

"No. Never mind. I don't know."

I expect Maribel to be angry that I'm not coming to the party, but when I tell her, she doesn't even look up from running a lint roller over her purple blazer. "Fine," she says, as if it doesn't matter.

But later on, when she's packing her bag, I catch her rubbing the back of her neck, as if she's just tallied up how much it's going to cost her when someone has to leave the party early because her toddler throws a tantrum.

⌒

Mrs. Arong is waiting outside the mall with Sophia when Mom drops me off a little before noon on Saturday. I had borrowed one of Maribel's purses, and before we get out of the car, Mom tucks a ten-dollar bill inside. "Maybe you can do a little shopping, too," she says with her news anchor's half-smile. I do my best to smile back.

When she sees us coming, Sophia springs off

the planter she's been sitting on. Mom and Mrs. Arong wave at each other.

"So I'll meet you back here in a few hours?" Mom asks me, glancing down at her watch.

"Yeah. I can call you when I'm ready."

"Oh, no, Sandra. Don't do that," Mrs. Arong says. "I'll give her a ride back home."

I can't let Mrs. Arong drive me home, because she and Sophia don't know where home actually is now. I always thought I'd get around to telling Sophia about losing the house and Dad being gone. About everything. But I never did.

It's just that every time I think about telling her, I imagine Sophia's reaction. Surprise, of course, but she'll feel sorry for me, too. Maybe even embarrassed.

I shake my head, just barely. Just enough, I hope, for Mom to notice.

She doesn't.

"Oh, would you?" she says. "That would be such a huge help. Griselda can show you the way."

"It's no trouble at all," Mrs. Arong says.

Mom kisses my forehead. "Have fun!" she says and walks back to Maribel's car. Mrs. Arong follows me and Sophia into the mall, then tells us we can wander around on our own.

"I'll meet you back here in two hours. Don't forget, Sophia: You need to find a dress for your Rita Moreno costume. Do you have your Living History costume figured out yet, Griselda? Please help Sophia. And *please* try to find some real food in here—not just junk."

We promise.

But the candy store is our first stop. We each take a cellophane bag and gaze at bins filled with red licorice ropes and rainbow-colored jawbreakers and pastel taffies. "If you weren't here, Mom wouldn't let me even *look* at this stuff," Sophia says.

I open a bin of gummy bears and pour just a few into my bag.

Sophia comes up behind me, snatches the bag, and adds another heaping scoop.

"But I can't—"

"My treat," she says. "Grandma sent birthday money."

Must be nice not having to worry about every penny, I think.

We stop inside an accessories store next. Sophia

tries on a pink fedora and then a sparking rhinestone tiara. I clip an artificial sunflower behind my ear.

"So cute!" Sophia says. "You should totally get that."

I pull out the clip and shake my head. "No. I don't think so." Cute isn't a good enough reason to spend money anymore. At least not for *me*.

Just as Sophia predicted, her mom isn't exactly *with* us. But she's never very far behind. I look over my shoulder now and then and, when Mrs. Arong sees me notice her, she turns away as if the nearest window display is the most interesting one she's ever seen.

I'm standing outside a department-store changing room where Sophia is finally trying on dresses. I spot Mrs. Arong behind a display of silk scarves.

Sophia steps out in time to see her, too. "Ugh. I know," she says. "So annoying. Just ignore her." She turns to face the mirror. "What do you think of this one?"

As usual, she doesn't give me a chance to answer.

"I mean, I *did* really want to be an Olympic

swimmer, but Rita Moreno turned out to be pretty interesting, too. She's this actress and singer, and she was the third person *ever* to win the Emmy, Grammy, Oscar, and Tony awards—all four of them. Do you think this is twirly enough?" She spins.

"I like it. Definitely twirlier than the last one." *If I were the one shopping, it wouldn't matter which was twirlier, just which one was cheaper.*

"Aren't you going to try anything on?"

"Ummm..." There isn't any point. I found one dress the same daffodil yellow as in Lady Bird Johnson's portrait, but it costs more than ten lip glosses—at full price.

I want to get out of here. "Hey, aren't you hungry?"

"Yes!" Sophia steps back into the changing room and closes the door. "Let me just pay for this and we'll go find something to eat."

The food court is at the other end of the mall. Mrs. Arong follows us there, always twenty steps behind. We make a slow lap, looking at all the menus and sampling bites of French fry and teri-yaki chicken along the way. Once we've checked everything out, Sophia orders two slices of cheese pizza and a giant cup of root beer. I settle for a warm pretzel. If it were listed in the Alma catalog, it would have been called Salty as the Sea. After paying with Mom's money, I grab a packet of mustard and a handful of napkins and sit down at the table where Sophia has already started eating.

On her wrist, along with the friendship bracelet I made her last year, is a silver bracelet with a dolphin charm. I hadn't noticed it before.

"That's so pretty," I say, pointing. "Is it new?"

She shakes her wrist and the charm clinks. "Birthday present. And I'm glad you like it because..." She takes a box out of her purse and gives it to me. "Open!"

Inside is a silver bracelet almost exactly like hers.

"We match! Sort of. Yours has a rose charm instead of a dolphin. Because of your garden, you know? Don't you want to put it on?"

I'm nodding. I'm holding out my wrist. I'm even saying thank you. But all I'm thinking is *I have nothing to give her.*

I can't believe I didn't bring her anything. I

open Maribel's purse and feel around inside. She always carries makeup—you never know when you might make a sale, after all. I pull out a box of lip gloss. Wicked Stepsister.

"Almost forgot," I say, sliding the box across the table. "Happy birthday to you, too. Sorry I, um, didn't wrap it."

Sophia squeals and claps. She opens the box, and the lip gloss, an electric orange-red, drops onto the table.

"It's from the Fairytale Collection," I say, trying to sound enthusiastic. "No one else at school has it yet. Exclusive."

Sophia doesn't lift her eyes from the table. "Thanks, Geez. It's…nice." She puts the lip gloss back in the box.

I know it's not a very good gift—not a silver bracelet, or even a bag of her favorite candy—but I don't think it's *that* bad, and anyway, it's the best I can do.

"What's wrong? Do you hate it?"

"No," she says, still staring at the box. "It's just…"

"*What?*"

She finally looks back at me. "It's like all you care about anymore is lipstick."

It isn't true. I don't care about lipstick. Or lip gloss. Or any of it. What I care about is having a home with two parents living in it. Like I used to. I miss the feeling of buying new clothes or lunch at the mall without worrying, without even thinking, about how much money it costs. I'm angry about the money I'm losing being at the mall instead of working with Maribel, and I'm angry about having to work with Maribel in the first place.

Sophia doesn't know any of this, so of course she can't understand how I feel. But for some reason that only makes it worse. She will *never* understand.

"Well, all *you* care about are your jelly beans and your dress and spending your mom's money!" I slam my hands on the table.

Sophia opens her mouth, but nothing comes out. Her cheeks turn bright red and tears pool in the corners of her eyes.

Oh, geez. I think I might throw up.

"Sophia, I'm so, *so* sorry. I didn't mean..."

Her face crumples, and she really starts crying. She pushes her fast-food tray away from her.

Mrs. Arong rushes over to the table. "Girls? What's going on?"

I look down at my shoes. "Can we leave?"

"I think we'd better," Mrs. Arong says.

꙳

Sophia sits in the front seat with her mom instead of in the back with me. I drop my candy bag on the floor mat, next to my feet. Just looking at it makes my stomach hurt all over again.

Mrs. Arong keeps trying to get us to talk. She asks Sophia about the dress she bought. She asks me how I'm liking Mrs. Ramos-McCaffrey's class. But when neither of us answers with more than a word or two, she finally gives up and turns on the radio.

I don't know what made me snap the way I did. With my forehead pressed against the window, I replay the conversation over and over in my mind. Sophia's squeaky laugh when I handed her my gift and the way her smile shriveled when she opened it. I squeeze my eyes shut, wishing I could crumple up the whole afternoon, toss it in a wastebasket, and start over. I unclasp the charm bracelet and leave it next to me on the seat. She probably wishes she had never given it to me.

Then I open my eyes and realize, too late to do anything about it, that Mrs. Arong has driven me to the wrong house.

It would have been the right house six months ago, but not anymore.

A man and a woman are outside in my garden, pulling weeds. A little girl with yellow pigtails holds a hose up to the strawberries, but mostly just drenches her shoes.

Parked alongside the curb, Mrs. Arong looks at me in the rearview mirror. "Griselda? Do you have . . . family visiting?"

I open my mouth and almost say yes. *Yes, those are my cousins in the garden. Thanks for the ride. See you later. Goodbye.*

Only, then what? What happens when Mrs. Arong wants to wait at the curb until I make it inside? Or what happens when she drives away and I'm left standing outside a stranger's house?

"Griselda?"

I can't avoid it anymore. I have to say something. I have to say it out loud.

I swallow. "We lost the house. It's not ours. We don't live here anymore."

"You lost..." Mrs. Arong doesn't understand, and then, suddenly, she does. "Oh, Griselda. Oh, *honey*. You should have told us." She's still looking at me in the rearview mirror, her eyes wider now.

Sophia unbuckles her seat belt and twists around. "You *what*?"

"Sophia—" Mrs. Arong tries to stop her, but she doesn't have to. It doesn't matter.

I look at Sophia and say it again. "We lost the house. We don't live here anymore."

"So where do you live? Are you homeless?"

"I don't think so," I say.

"Sophia, enough," Mrs. Arong says. Then quieter, to me, "Well, Griselda, where should we take you?"

⌒⌒

I fling open the door and jump out of the Arongs' car without saying goodbye. I storm past Mom, who's outside checking the mailbox, where there's probably yet another overdue bill.

From the kitchen window, I see her wave and walk over to the car. Mrs. Arong rolls down her window, reaches out, and takes one of Mom's hands between both of hers.

Mom tilts her head. I can't see her face, but I know her lips are pressed into a sad half-smile. *Trust me. This is not as bad as it sounds.*

At school on Monday morning, Logan brings me the bag of candy with the silver bracelet inside.

"Sophia asked me to give this to you."

There's a note taped to the bag:

You forgot this in the car. Also, I'm sorry about everything. I didn't know. You could have told me. Love, Sophia.

"She's right," Logan says. "You could have told us."

"But you already know everything."

"Not really. Not from you."

I decide to find Sophia at lunch and try to

explain it all. But when I get to the cafeteria, she's already sitting with Daisy, and it doesn't look as if there's room for me. Instead, I carry my tray over to Kennedy Castro's table and open up the new Alma catalog.

CHAPTER THIRTEEN

So much of what happens in life is out of your
control, but how you respond to it is in your
control. That's what I try to remember.

—HILLARY RODHAM CLINTON

"It's a guppy."

"And I named her after you," Logan says.
"Happy birthday."

I had gone to his house to drop off a blue suit
coat that used to belong to Grandpa. After watching Logan turn my empty Alma boxes into a home
for Magdalena, I thought maybe he could use
Grandpa's old coat to make his Lafayette costume.
Nana didn't mind. She liked the idea.

"Come in for a minute," Logan had said, grinning when he answered the door. "I have a surprise for you." That's when he unveiled Griselda the Guppy.

She swims lazily in a shallow dish at the bottom of Magdalena's aquarium. She has no idea what's coming.

"You got me a guppy."

"Cool, right?"

"It's a guppy that's about to become snake food."

"I know! Look, here comes Magdalena."

"Actually, I should get going. Mom made a cake. You could come over?" I stop and start again. "I mean, it would be fun if you could come over and celebrate with us. Do you want to?" It's the first time I've invited him to Nana's house since we moved in. He must know it, too, but he doesn't make a big deal about it. I like that about Logan.

"In a minute. You're missing the best part, you know."

"It's not the best part if you're the guppy."

"True."

"It was nice knowing you, Griselda."

When I first see it there, I don't think there's anything unusual about Mom's car being parked on the street in front of Nana's house. Then I remember who's been driving Mom's car. I jump off Logan's front porch and run to Nana's yard.

"Dad?"

He is standing outside, hands in his pockets, staring at the mint patch. He's wearing rumpled blue jeans, and his plaid collared shirt is untucked. He holds an arm out for a hug, maybe an invitation, maybe a request. I don't respond to either.

"What are you doing here?"

He drops his arm. "It's your birthday. Aren't you happy to see me?"

Finally, I wrap my arms around his waist. "Of course I am. It's just that I didn't know you were coming."

"I didn't want to say anything, in case..." He doesn't finish his sentence.

"In case something came up?"

He crosses his arms and looks away, over at the mint again.

"Does Mom know you're here?" I lower my voice. "Does Maribel?"

Just then, my sister calls out the window, "Are you guys gonna be out there all day or what?"

Dad sighs. "She knows. They're all waiting for us. Shall we go inside?"

Mom and Maribel, Nana and Tía Carla are all in the kitchen. Dad joins them, sitting down at the table with a yawn.

"So, what do you think of your big surprise?" Mom asks, setting down a cake with twelve unlit candles and a cluster of buttercream roses at the center.

She stops and looks around.

"Wait, where's Logan? Isn't he coming?"

"He's waiting for Magdalena to finish her dinner."

Nana shudders.

"Maybe we should start with presents, then," Mom suggests.

Dad stands and retrieves a gift from on top of the kitchen counter.

I loosen the ribbon and unwrap a new pair of gardening gloves—nice ones with tiny rubber dots on the palms to help with grip.

I slide my hand into one and open and close my fist. "Thanks," I say, looking at Mom.

"I asked your dad to pick them out for you. I haven't seen any of your old gardening things in a while, and I thought maybe your gloves got lost in...all the confusion."

I glance at Maribel. She rolls her eyes, which makes me smile.

I reach across the table and squeeze Dad's hand. "Thank you. And thanks for bringing them all this way."

Next, Tía Carla gives me a package of hot-pink hair chalk.

"Tranquila, Sandra, it washes right out," Tía Carla says as Mom's eyebrows start to wrinkle and a whine of protest squirms out of her lips.

"I *am* calm. I was just going to say, maybe you and Sophia can try it out together, Griselda."

"Or you and Logan," Maribel teases.

I chuck the gloves at her, but she dodges and they hit the wall.

Nana gives me a new teacup. Hillary Clinton. Mint green with a sprig of violets.

Finally, when I've finished opening everything

else, Maribel reaches behind her back and pulls out a long, slender box.

"Lip gloss?" I pick it up off the table and shake it.

"Oh, Geez. Just open it," Maribel grumbles. "You're as bad as Nana."

Nana swats her playfully on the back of the head.

I tear apart the paper and open the box. It's the rose-gold watch, the prize from Maribel's Alma rewards booklet.

"I thought you were selling it," I say, lifting the watch out of the box.

"Changed my mind. So are you going to wear it, or just look at it?" She reaches over and helps me with the clasp.

When Logan arrives, they all sing "Happy Birthday." I blow out my candles and wish the only wish I have anymore: that things go back to the way they were. And with Dad home, it almost feels as though it could come true. Until I remember that he's leaving again, first thing in the morning.

Later on, while Mom and Dad wash up, I go outside to walk Logan back home and to water the plants. The mint patch, I notice, has swallowed even more of the yard. We never would have let this happen in the garden back at our old house.

One morning, the summer after I turned nine, Dad and I got up early, while the air outside was still cool and wet. We mowed the front lawn extra short, then smothered what was left of the grass under newspaper and compost. "We'll let the sun do the rest," Dad had said.

Lying in bed that night, my shoulders all sunburned and achy, I thought about how the grass used to feel, warm and scratchy between my bare toes. Then I thought about how we were killing it, how probably, the sun had already baked it brown and dry. I worried we had made an enormous mistake, one it was too late to fix.

But the next morning, before he left for work, Dad gave me a pencil and a stack of graph paper from his office. He told me to sketch out some ideas for the new garden we would plant where the lawn used to be.

On those fresh, blank pages, covered in neat blue squares, every beautiful thing seemed possible. I started with a border of tidy hedges, rosemary and lavender with gray-green leaves and purple flowers. They would smell fresh and bright, a little like pine trees almost, only softer.

Inside the hedges, I drew planter boxes. In spring, they would be filled with daffodils and tulips, stretching toward the sun. In summer, strawberries would spill over their redwood edges.

And at the center of it all, I imagined roses, as many colors as we could fit: from pearly-white Snowdrift, to ballet-slipper Kiss Me, to sunny-yellow Midas Touch.

We planted the roses in September. In June, Mom and I made our first batch of strawberry jam.

Maybe none of it is mine anymore. But I still have a chance to get at least some of it back. I go to my room to line up another week's worth of lip gloss.

CHAPTER FOURTEEN

I was allowed to progress in the business
world as fast and as far as I could.
—FLORENCE HARDING

All through the rest of November, the contest deadline nags like a rock in my shoe. I can hardly stop
thinking about it.

The pressure—and the weeks of practice—
make me braver, at least. I'm not so red-faced and
shaky when I have to talk to people. Some days I
sell four, five—even six glosses. But other days only
two or three, and I start to worry I'll be out of the
competition before it even begins.

Then November winds down, and everything else speeds up.

Maribel books makeup parties weekend after weekend, sometimes two on the same day. In exchange for free babysitting, she agrees to credit any lip gloss sales to me.

Customers at school start adding presents for their friends and relatives to their regular purchases for themselves. They give me one of my most successful ideas yet: selling to parents.

"Lip gloss makes a great gift," I tell two moms leaning against a van while they wait for their kids after school. "I know *I* would love to find these in my stocking."

They buy every tube left in my backpack and take home brochures to order more.

By the middle of December, with a week left of school before winter break, only five more paper links still hang from the back of my closet door. Only fifty more tubes of lip gloss, and I'll qualify for a chance to become the Fresh New Face of Alma and, more important, to win the five-thousand-dollar cash prize.

The day is almost over. Mrs. Ramos-McCaffrey is reviewing a science test. I'm thinking about how I'm so close now that maybe I should call Dad and tell him. Maybe he'd come home again—and stay this time—if he knew there was hope of starting over.

An office assistant comes in with a note for Mrs. Ramos-McCaffrey. She takes a break from the review to read it, then looks up. At me.

"Griselda, Dr. Keckley would like to see you in her office."

"Oooooh," tease voices from behind me.

"That's enough," Mrs. Ramos-McCaffrey says. "Geez, why don't you pack up your things in case the bell rings before the two of you are finished."

The principal's office. I have never been called to the principal's office in my life. My cheeks burn as I gather my papers into a folder and follow the assistant down the hall.

Through a window into the office, I see the back of a familiar head, red-black hair almost, but not quite, skimming her shoulders. This is even worse than I thought. Mom.

The assistant clears her throat, trying to get my

attention so that I'll walk through the door she's been holding open. I swallow hard and step into the office.

Mom is talking to Mr. Singh, another one of the teachers. She's smiling, at least. That's a good sign. Only it's her pressed-lip half-smile, so I can't tell whether she means it or not.

"Oh, I'm flattered, but I haven't been in the business for years. I'm not sure I have very much to offer, but if you think it would be helpful, then of course I'll come talk with your journalism class. Just give me a call."

Mr. Singh thanks her and leaves the office carrying a pile of essays.

Mom's smile vanishes the second he does.

"Griselda, what is this about? The school called Tía Carla's salon asking me to come down to the principal's office? What's going on?"

I have a feeling it must have something to do with the makeup, but I don't know how or where to begin.

Just then, Dr. Keckley's door opens. "Good. You're both here. Why don't you come in and have a seat?" She wears her hair in twists, dark brown with streaks of silver, that fall to her chin, and she has a different pantsuit for every day of the year. Today's is turquoise.

On one wall of Dr. Keckley's office, three diplomas hang one on top of the other in oak frames. The opposite wall is papered over with pictures of former El Dorado School students dressed in their high school graduation gowns. I look for a picture of Maribel until I remember we didn't order portraits last year. And even if we had, Maribel isn't sentimental enough to have sent one back to her elementary school principal.

Dr. Keckley pulls out a chair for Mom, who gives me one more questioning look as she sits down. *I don't know*, I mouth before sitting down next to her.

Dr. Keckley looks at Mom, then at me. When neither of us says anything, she claps her hands together under her chin and leans across the desk.

"Mrs. Zaragoza, I'm getting the sense you don't know what this is about."

Mom meets her gaze and leans forward, too. "You're right. I have absolutely no idea what this is about."

I have to look away. On a corner of her desk, Dr. Keckley keeps a jade plant. Its leaves are dropping off—overwatered, I guess. People are always over-watering their succulents.

"Griselda is doing well in her classes, isn't she? I know I haven't been paying as close attention as I used to—I've had, well...a lot on my mind. But she gets her homework done, and I always check her progress reports, and—"

"Oh, it's nothing like that." Dr. Keckley stops her, shaking her head and leaning back. "Griselda is a bright student and, as usual, her teacher has nothing but good things to say about her work."

Mrs. Ramos-McCaffrey has been talking about me?

"And she hasn't gotten into any trouble." This time, Mom isn't asking; she's telling. The only time I've ever been in trouble over my behavior was in second grade—for talking in class. Only, I wasn't the one talking; it was Sophia. Still, Mrs. Ross said neither of us was paying attention, and that afternoon, we both had to scrub cafeteria tables while everyone else played at recess.

Dr. Keckley swivels in her chair. "Well, no, I suppose Griselda hasn't broken any rules. Not exactly. Quite frankly, it didn't occur to me that we needed a rule for this particular situation."

"Then, what?"

"Well, it's sensitive. You see, I received a call from a parent this morning. Her daughter has been going without lunch several times a week. She's understandably concerned."

Dr. Keckley pauses and looks at me. I'm beginning to see where this conversation is going, but Mom still doesn't.

"I'd be concerned, too," Mom says, looking from me to Dr. Keckley. "But what does it have to do with Griselda? *She's* eating, isn't she?"

Dr. Keckley sighs. "It seems the reason this student has been going without lunch is that she has been saving her lunch money in order to purchase cosmetics—from your daughter."

"*What?* From Maribel?"

"No, from Griselda. Now, I realize this might be a...*sensitive* subject. We know that Griselda is eligible for free lunch this year, and that your family has moved in with her grandmother?"

Mom narrows her eyes and nods. Her perfect

mask of calm and steady reassurance begins to melt away.

"Of course, I cannot pretend to understand the financial stress and strain you must be under," Dr. Keckley goes on.

"There have been some...changes," Mom says. "But we're doing just fine. *Griselda* is fine."

"Certainly there has been more pressure at home?" Dr. Keckley asks.

"Maybe. But Griselda has always been resilient and responsible and—"

"Ah." Dr. Keckley points at Mom as if she's finally landed on the right answer. "And I think it's perfectly appropriate for a child Griselda's age to have some responsibilities around the house— washing the dishes, for example, or even preparing a simple dinner one or two nights a week. However, I don't believe she should be asked to contribute to the household's *income*. She is, after all, still a child."

Mom slaps a hand over her mouth, and her face flushes as red as mine.

Then she closes her eyes, takes a deep breath in

through her nose, holds for three beats, then blows it out through her mouth. By the time she opens her eyes again, the mask is back.

I start trying to explain, but Mom clamps her hand over my shoulder, shushing me.

"Dr. Keckley," she says in her serious but soothing voice. "I can assure you that my husband and I have *not* put our twelve-year-old daughter to work selling makeup. I am beginning to understand what must have happened here, and I *will* put a stop to it."

"Thank you. That's all I need to hear. As I said, Griselda hasn't done anything wrong, not *exactly*. But I must ask that she stop selling cosmetics at school—it has become something of a distraction."

Mom puts her purse back on her shoulder and stands. "That I can promise."

"Just one more thing before you go?"

Mom sits down again.

"If you find you need any resources, some extra help during what must be a *challenging* time—"

Mom smiles her sad half-smile. "No. I appreciate the offer, but as *I* said, we're doing just fine, thank you."

Mom is silent as we leave the school building, and she walks so fast I have to scamper to keep up.

The afternoon bell had rung while we were still in Dr. Keckley's office, and outside, students are already lining up in front of buses or tossing their backpacks into the trunks of their parents' cars. Beth jogs over when she sees me, six dollars clutched in her fist. I shake my head. "Not today," I tell her, then walk a little faster to catch up to Mom. Behind me, Beth calls, "Wait! What's going on?"

I wonder if Mom meant it about me not selling makeup anymore and if there's anything I can say to change her mind. I can't stop now, not when I'm so close.

When we get to Maribel's car, Mom unlocks the passenger door, then walks around to hers, stopping to take another deep breath and blow it out again before opening her door. Inside, she drops her head to her chest and rubs her temples.

"Griselda, I have never been so embarrassed. The idea that I would put you to work...that you would take someone's lunch money."

"Mom, no, it's not like that, I—"

She doesn't let me finish.

"No," she says, talking over me and sitting up straight again. "Maribel is going to have to explain herself." She pulls her seat belt across her chest, puts on a pair of sunglasses, and we drive off.

CHAPTER FIFTEEN

What in this world can compensate for the
sympathy and confidence of a mother and
a sister.

—Dolley Madison

Inside Belleza, Tía Carla—her hair ironed stick
straight and dyed bluish-black—is standing behind
a client, suggesting a cut and color to frame the
woman's heart-shaped face.

Tía Carla spots me in the mirror and waves her
fingers, still consulting her client. But when she
sees Mom's face, she excuses herself and hurries
over, blocking our path.

"Sandra?" she asks, smiling but with an eyebrow raised. "Is something the matter?"

Mom steps around her. "Where is Maribel?"

She doesn't need to wait for Tía Carla's answer. Maribel's voice, steady and sure, rings out from the nail lounge.

"Our new top coat, Forever After, was designed *specifically* with working professionals like you in mind. Alma's miracle formula seals your polish and protects your manicure against the wear and tear of everyday living."

Mom's pace quickens. "Maribel!" Her voice is as loud and raw as I have ever heard it.

Tía Carla and I chase her into the nail lounge where my sister is applying the new top coat to a woman's thumbnail. She stops mid-brushstroke when she sees Mom.

"Maribel," Mom says again. This time her voice is low, icy, and somehow even more dangerous than when she had raised it just a few moments earlier.

The customers in the nail lounge look away uncomfortably, but I can tell they're curious, too, wondering what's going on and what will happen next.

I try again to get Mom's attention. "Mom, if you would just let me explain—"

"Not now, Griselda." Mom turns to Maribel. "Would you like to tell me why the school principal just accused me of making my youngest daughter sell makeup to support her family?"

"But, Mom, she didn't say—"

"Griselda, *not now!*" Mom waves me away. "Well, Maribel, what do you have to say for yourself?"

Maribel twists the top back onto the bottle of nail polish and puts it down gently on the manicure table. She looks up and says casually, "I say, talk to Griselda."

"Griselda is a child, your baby sister. And I cannot believe you would put her to work for you. If you insist on wasting your time and your talent on this...*makeup*, you can either start paying your nana some rent or you can move out. What you absolutely *cannot* do is drag Griselda into it."

Maribel stands. She's not so calm and casual

anymore. "Why do you *think* I'm doing this? To move out!"

Moving out? I thought she was trying to win a car.

Mom looks startled for a second, but not enough to stop. She shakes her head. "But to take advantage of your little sister like this? I have never known you to be so selfish."

I've heard enough. Maribel may be impatient and demanding. But the one thing she hasn't been through all of this is selfish. She's the only one who has helped me.

"Mom!" I say, raising my voice so loud that it doesn't sound like mine anymore. "Would you *please* listen?"

Not just Mom, but everyone else in the room turns to look at me.

"I'm *not* a baby. Maribel didn't make me do *anything*. This was all *my* idea."

Mom squints as though she's trying to make sense of a complicated instruction manual. Then she sinks into one of the manicure chairs. "*Your* idea? What do you mean it was *your* idea?"

Tía Carla presses her hands down on my shoulders and squeezes, partly to calm me down, but mostly to shut me up. "Ladies, let's take this into my office, shall we? *Now?*"

She leads us up a narrow staircase and unlocks her office door. Maribel scoops a handful of candy-coated sunflower seeds from a bowl on Tía Carla's desk, then leans against a bookshelf. Mom and I sit on opposite ends of a navy-blue couch.

All of us sit there, waiting for someone to say something. It reminds me of that afternoon—Mom and Dad, me and Maribel in the living room on West Mariposa Avenue. I remember Dad's words. *Game over.*

"But I'm so close!" I plead, as if he's sitting right next to me. I think about everything I've lost in the past year: my house, my garden, even my best friend. I can't lose this chance, too. "Don't make me give up now."

"Griselda," Mom says. "Please, *please* tell me what's going on."

So I do.

I tell her I know we're better off than a lot of other people—we have a place to live and enough to eat— but that my chest goes all tight every time there's a field trip, a costume, or new school supplies to pay for.

I try to explain the standing-on-my-tiptoes-but-still-can't-reach feeling of not being able to buy a birthday present for my best friend.

I tell her about the contest and the five thousand dollars, about wanting to help and wanting to win again.

"Dad left to make a fresh start. Well, maybe with that prize money, we can have a fresh start right here."

Tía Carla and Maribel creep out of the office. It's so quiet I can hear the music, all muffled, playing downstairs in the salon. Mom doesn't say anything for a while.

Then, almost whispering, she asks, "Why didn't you tell me?"

"Why didn't you tell *me*?"

"Tell you what?"

"*Anything*. About Dad's business? About our house? About the truck?"

Mom folds her hands in her lap and drops her chin to her chest. I suspect she's putting on her sad-sweet half-smile, but when she lifts her head again, she's frowning. A real and honest frown.

"Oh, I don't know, Griselda. I think it was partly

because I didn't want to believe it was happening myself," she says. "But mostly it was because I didn't want to worry you."

"I'd rather be worried and try to do something about it than be the only one who doesn't know what's going on."

Mom slides closer to me. "I sometimes forget what a fighter you are, in your own way. It's what your name means, you know?'"

I know. She's only told me a million times. "I wish you had given me a beautiful name. Like Maribel's." *At least I wouldn't have lost that.*

Mom reaches over and brushes my bangs out of my eyes. "Hmm. Maribel does have a beautiful name. I was so young when she was born, and that was all that mattered to me. I had grown up by the time I had you, and I wanted you to have a name that was beautiful because it was also strong."

$$\sim$$

Mom says Maribel and I have to chip in to take Grandpa's car for a tune-up and oil change since we've been using it so often. After that, I can keep the rest of my earnings—in a bank account, though, not in a box under the bed. I can still babysit, too, she says. But I can't sell any more makeup. She won't budge on that, not even an inch.

$$\sim$$

Late that night, with only the dim hallway light still on, I kick off my blankets and pummel my pillow as though wrestling with the bedding will help me fall asleep.

Maribel rolls over. "You know, I was wondering what you wanted all that money for."

"Doesn't matter now."

"I thought maybe you were trying to save enough to buy our house back. I didn't want to be the one to have to break it to you."

"I'm not stupid, Maribel, and I'm not a baby."

"I know you're not."

She stops talking, but I can tell from her breathing that she hasn't gone back to sleep.

"I thought you were trying to win that convertible," I say.

"The Alma-mobile? No. As long as Nana keeps letting me borrow the Crown Victoria, I don't need another car. What I *need* is to get out of this house and into college like I planned."

"But why? Why can't you go to college here? What's wrong with community college? Is it just because it's what Mom wants that you won't go?"

"That's not it," Maribel says. "Community college is great—maybe I'll end up going to one. But I don't feel like myself here. This isn't where I'm supposed to be."

⌒

When I wake up the next morning, an Alma Cosmetics order form is resting on my nightstand: fifty Fairytale Collection lip glosses, in assorted colors. Charged to Carla Palomares, Salon Belleza.

CHAPTER SIXTEEN

I always did like the unexpected and am
waiting with intense interest the next jump.
—GRACE COOLIDGE

Kennedy and Ava still make room for me at their
lunch table when we go back to school after winter break. But without the Alma catalog, I feel even
more out of place sitting with them than I ever did
before. After two awkward lunch periods, I go back
to my old table in the corner.

"What, no nail polish? No lipstick?" Logan
says, sitting down across from me.

"Not anymore."

"What happened?"

I gulp down a big drink of milk, wipe my mouth, and tell him the whole story.

"Whoa," he says at the end of it. "So your aunt saved the day? Do you really think you can win, though?"

"Why? Do you think I won't?"

"No. It just doesn't seem like you, that's all. You never want to be the center of attention."

"Well, maybe this is the fresh new face of Griselda Zaragoza."

A few weeks later, the letter arrives. Nana gives it to me as soon as I get home that afternoon, before I'm even all the way through the door. Purple confetti flutters onto the kitchen floor when I open it.

Congratulations!

Your exemplary sales place you among the elite ranks of young people from throughout the country who truly embody the Soul of Beauty.

As a Fresh New Face finalist, we are pleased to invite you to attend this year's Alma Expo, with all expenses paid. As always, the Expo will be held at the Regal Hotel in our nation's capital.

You will be an honored guest at the annual Soul of Beauty Brunch, where you'll celebrate the Fairytale Collection, mix and mingle with our top-selling associates—and compete to become the Fresh New Face of Alma Cosmetics.

Please prepare a speech, no more than five minutes in length, on the person who, for you, best represents the Spirit of Success.

I put the letter down. It's official: I did it. Nana is smiling at me, her hands clasped nervously in front of her.

I try to smile back. "I'm in." But I'm not as excited as I thought I'd be.

A five-minute speech. In front of all the top-selling associates. In front of all the other finalists. When I think about it that way, five minutes sounds like forever.

Possibly the best thing I've learned so far about Lady Bird Johnson is that she was the top student at her high school until she let her grades slip—on purpose. She did it because the student with the best grades had to make a speech at graduation, and she hated public speaking that much.

It probably shouldn't surprise me that the Fresh New Face of Alma Cosmetics is also supposed to say something. I just wasn't expecting a speech.

But five minutes isn't actually forever, I tell myself.

Five minutes is shorter than a visit to the dentist. It's faster than I can run a mile in PE.

Five minutes is longer than I've seen my dad in weeks, and that means I just have to do it.

"Are Mom and Maribel here? I want to show them."

"Maribel just left, and your mother hasn't come home from the salon yet, but she should be back soon." Nana kisses my forehead. "Congratulations, mija."

I take the letter to the bedroom to leave it on the desk where Maribel will find it.

Living with Nana is the first time we've ever had to share a bedroom. With Maribel saving money all these months, she must have almost enough to move out. Mom's old room is going to feel so empty without her in it.

Back when we first made our deal, half my

profits seemed like a lot to trade for Maribel's signature on the Alma entry form. Worth it, but a lot.

Now I think I owe her so much more than that for all the advice she's given me and all the car rides we've shared. Maybe it's been a long time since I locked myself into that bathroom on the first day of kindergarten, but Maribel is still getting me unstuck.

I unfold my letter and smooth it out on her desk. That's when I notice the purple confetti. Another letter, printed on the same lavender stationery as the one I just opened, peeks out from under one of Maribel's notepads. I slide it out.

Congratulations!
    Your exemplary sales place you among the elite ranks of young people from throughout the country who truly embody the Soul of Beauty.

Oh, I think. *They wanted Maribel to have a copy of my letter, too.*

I'm such a baby sometimes.

Half a second later I realize how silly that sounds and how silly I have been.

Silly to think the fresh new face of Alma Cosmetics could be anyone's but Maribel's. Least of all mine.

Her name literally means beautiful.

Of course the letter is hers. Of course she entered the contest, too. My heart thuds so loudly I'm sure Nana can hear it from the kitchen. I take both letters to my bed and lie down.

Silly to think Maribel believed in me. Everything she did, she did to help herself.

The more I sell, the more money you make.

I stay there on the bed, staring at my Lady Bird Johnson teacup until Maribel gets back.

"Geez! You scared me," she says, holding her hand over her chest and letting her makeup bag fall to the floor with a thud. "Why are you sitting in the dark?" She flicks the light on. "Congratulations, by the way. Nana said a letter came from Alma? You're a finalist?"

I hold up my letter.

Then hers.

"Congratulations to you, too."

She collapses into the desk chair. "Oh, Geez, I'm so sorry."

"You've been competing against me this whole time?"

"No, of course not. I've been trying to *help* you. It's just that I could really use that money, and I didn't think—"

"You didn't think I could do it?"

"I didn't think it mattered so much to you. But now I know, and I'm dropping out."

"So you can tell everyone you let your baby sister win? No way. Better idea: I'll win without any more of your *help*."

I have less than a month to prepare—not just to give a speech, but to take on Maribel. I'll have to be flawless to even stand a chance.

Mom and Nana take me to the mall, where I spend a little of my Alma money on a winter coat and something new to wear to the Soul of Beauty Brunch. The first dress I take off the rack is long, floaty, and floral, and exactly what I would have picked a year ago.

"Qué linda," Nana says.

"Do you want to try it on?" Mom asks.

It's pretty, and I almost say yes. Almost. Then I try to imagine the dress on Maribel and can't.

"Nope." I hang it back up and keep looking.

Finally, standing in front of the dressing room mirror in a plain gray skirt, a white blouse buttoned up to my neck, and a lavender cardigan, I nod. "This is it."

"Are you sure?" Mom says. "It's very... serious."

"Professional?"

"Mmm... grown-up."

"Then it's perfect. Next, shoes."

I try on a pair of black pumps, shiny as mirrors, with two-inch heels and straps around the ankles. They're snug, but not tight. "These feel good."

Then I stand up.

I'm not used to walking in anything besides my white school sneakers. I wobble and almost fall, clinging to Nana's shoulder for balance.

"I think maybe you should try some flats instead," Mom says, looking over the rows of shoes. She holds up a pair with pointy toes. "These are nice. They look comfortable, too. *And* they're on sale."

I picture Maribel about to knock on a stranger's

door, makeup satchel slung over her shoulder. She stands straight and *tall*.

"No, I'll take the heels."

"You don't want to stumble on your way to the podium."

"I won't stumble. I'll practice."

When we get home, I walk back and forth across Nana's kitchen, my shoes *click-clacking* on the tile floor, until it's time for dinner.

Every day after school, I change into the heels and practice walking up and down the front porch steps, and even across the driveway to Logan's house.

"You should try playing basketball in those shoes," he says one afternoon. "That'd be real good practice."

If I wasn't worried about scuffing them, I would. I can*not* fall down.

On my way back to Nana's door, I stop to look at the mint patch again. It's in a sunny spot, perfect for an herb garden, if only I could figure out what to do about that mint.

On the night before my flight, I unpack all the clothes I've been storing in my suitcase and replace them with the ones I'll be taking to Washington, DC.

"Need some help?" Mom asks, leaning against the bedroom door. She's been following me around the house all day, and I keep expecting her to tell me she's changed her mind and I can't go after all. She doesn't, though.

"I can handle it."

Then Maribel steps into the doorway, and Mom moves aside to let her through.

"Hey," she says.

"Hey."

"I'll leave you girls to it," Mom says, turning around and walking back down the hall.

I still want to be mad at Maribel for lying to me about the contest. But if she hadn't entered, if she hadn't qualified as a finalist, I might not have been able to go. If you're under eighteen, a parent is supposed to accompany you to the Alma Expo. Only, parents have to pay for their own airplane tickets, which I didn't even bother asking Mom about. As a finalist, Maribel's ticket is covered. We arrange it with the Alma people that she'll be my guardian for the weekend.

She goes to the closet and takes dresses and jackets off hangers. She folds her clothes and places everything in neat stacks on her bed, then fills little zippered pouches with makeup, soap, shampoo, toothpaste. On her nightstand, a notepad is opened to a checklist. Every time she adds something to a pouch, she draws a line through another item on the list.

I finish packing before she does, zip up my suitcase, and prop it against the wall next to the door. I go to the living room—where Mom's been sleeping on a fold-out couch—to call Dad.

I want him to know that the speech I wrote for the Soul of Beauty Brunch is all about him. It's about how, once upon a time, just like Lady Bird Johnson, he took a small business and turned it into a big one. Maybe he didn't become a millionaire like she did, but at least we didn't worry about money.

And the story isn't over. That's what I really want them to know. The trees Dad planted are still growing. There's still a street sign out there with our name on it.

I leave out the parts about owing money and leaving town, because we're going to rewrite all of that.

But when Dad answers the phone, he sounds so tired and faraway that I change my mind.

"I'm all packed for the trip. I just wanted to call and say bye."

"You girls have a great time. Take lots of pictures. I can't wait to see them."

But when will he see us in person, I want to ask.

"Dad?"

"Hmm?"

"You know that spot out in Nana's backyard where all the mint is growing?"

"Sure. Why?"

"I was thinking it would be a good place for an herb garden."

There's a pause, and then Dad says, "You're probably right. Gets good sun."

"But I don't know what to do about all that mint. It's out of control. Nothing else can grow there."

"You'll find a way, Griselda," he says. "You always figure it out."

CHAPTER SEVENTEEN

Had I stepped into Noah's Ark, I do not think I
could have been more utterly astonished.
—Louisa Adams

Every two minutes, it seems, from the time we pull
out of Nana's driveway until we turn into the parking lot at the airport, Mom warns Maribel, "Don't
take your eyes off your sister!" Then she turns to
me. "Don't wander away from your sister!"

"*Mom*," Maribel moans, throwing open the
trunk to pull out our bags. "Relax. Nothing's going
to happen to Geez."

Nana hooks her arm through mine and walks

with me to the terminal. "That girl doesn't stop," she whispers. "Make sure she feeds you."

"*Nana*. We'll be *fine*."

Maribel and I check our suitcases and wave to Mom and Nana as an escalator carries us toward our boarding gate. Mom cups her hands around her mouth. "You two take care of each other!"

Once we're on the plane with our seat belts pulled across our laps, I can almost forget that we aren't just taking off on a family vacation, with Mom and Dad sitting a row behind.

I reach down to get my headphones from my backpack. But when I see Maribel studying her Expo itinerary, I take mine out, too.

Opening ceremonies are tonight.

"We should try to go if we get to the hotel in time," Maribel says, tapping a pen against her teeth.

The Soul of Beauty Brunch is on Saturday morning, and there are all kinds of workshops on the schedule for later that afternoon. We can go to any we want. Maribel draws circles around two of them: "From Pastime to Full-Time: Your Career

Is in Your Hands!" and "Hidden Beauty: Finding New Customers Where You'd Least Expect."

I fall asleep to the soft rustle of Maribel flipping through her papers, then jolt awake hours later when the plane wheels hit the landing strip in Washington, DC.

Foggy-headed, I stretch in the aisle and follow Maribel off the plane. She's tied a purple scarf to her black makeup satchel, and I train my eyes on it as she winds her way through the concourse, down to the baggage claim area, and outside to the hotel shuttle stop. We pass a food court along the way, and I yell ahead at her to stop for a snack. She doesn't stop. She doesn't even slow down.

"Geez. Come on," she calls back. "We don't want to be late."

Nana tried to warn me, I think as I scamper to catch up.

⟨◦⟩

Our room is on the ninth floor of the redbrick hotel. Maribel lets me have the bed nearest the window so I can look out onto the street below. Even though it's cold, and even though the sunlight is beginning to fade, crowds of people—carrying newspapers, carrying cameras, carrying briefcases—stream over the sidewalk. Maribel tosses me one of the bean-and-potato burritos Nana packed us this morning and locks herself in the bathroom to change and freshen her makeup for the Alma Expo.

On the itinerary, the opening ceremonies are marked *Casual! We know you've been traveling!* so I stay dressed in the wooly green sweater and blue jeans I wore on the plane. I splash some water on my face, though, and rebraid my hair.

Swallowing the last bite of smooshed burrito as Maribel comes out of the bathroom, I start to realize I haven't done enough. Maribel is wearing a lilac blouse and a suit I recognize from Mom's closet. Her hair is pulled back into a sleek, low ponytail, and she's pinning one of Nana's old brooches onto her lapel.

"Let's go."

I look down at my sweater and jeans. "Should I change?"

"No time," Maribel says briskly. Maribel is never late.

Before we can get to the hotel ballroom, where

the opening ceremonies are about to start, we have to wait in a long, looping line that coils like a snake with a million violet scales. I might be the only person on the whole floor—maybe in the whole *hotel*—who isn't wearing some shade of purple.

Maribel fits right in. When I first saw her in Mom's old suit, she seemed smaller to me somehow. Like she was playing dress-up. But now, with her candy-apple smile back on, she just looks like one more flower in this purple bouquet.

Finally, we make it to the front of the line.

"Zaragoza and Zaragoza," Maribel tells a woman sitting behind the registration table.

The lady's fingers fly over a file full of yellow folders. She pulls two of them out.

"Ah, two of our Fresh New Face finalists! Congratulations. These are your registration packets. You'll find your name badges inside. I just know you'll find this an inspiring weekend. Best of luck tomorrow!"

She waves over the next woman in line before Maribel and I can thank her.

We find some space away from the crowd to open the envelopes and take out our badges. I slip a lanyard over my head. GRISELDA ZARAGOZA, JUNIOR ASSOCIATE. I'm sort of surprised it doesn't say GEEZ.

The lights inside the ballroom are dimmed, except for onstage, where a spotlight casts a lonely, lavender glow. Maribel leads us to two empty seats.

Just as we're sitting down, the spotlight goes dark. The audience gasps. I grab Maribel's hand. She squeezes mine back.

When the light switches on again, a woman wearing an evening gown covered in a dazzle of purple sequins stands onstage. I catch only a glimpse of her because, in a moment, everyone on the floor jumps to their feet and starts cheering.

The woman's voice, rich and velvety, pours out of the overhead speakers.

"You!" she sings. "Are the soul of beauty!" Silvery streamers and purple balloons rain down from the ceiling. The applause swells to a roar.

My stomach growls. The burrito hadn't been enough.

I look around for food and spot a long table at the back of the room with a lemonade fountain and piles of cookies.

I pull on Maribel's sleeve to get her attention.

I point to the table and point to my stomach. She leans over to say something. I can barely hear her, even though she's yelling right in my ear. "Come straight back! Mom'll never forgive me if I lose you on the first day."

I weave through the cheering crowd, stepping on toes and tripping over handbags. But no one seems to notice as the speech continues. When I get to the refreshments table, I resist the urge to take more than two cookies.

I would have gone right back to our seats, but the floral centerpieces on the table distract me, even in the low light. A bowlful of peonies with petals like ballet skirts fluttering in midleap. Creamy orchids with amethyst centers bursting above the edges of a crystal vase.

Partly because of the flowers, but also because I'm so tired, my mind drifts.

I yelp when Maribel taps on my shoulder. "Geez! Where were you? You said you'd come right back."

"Sorry."

"Well, I found you, anyway. Let's go."

Outside the violet chaos of the ballroom, the

hotel seems eerily still and quiet. "You didn't want to stay until the end?"

Maribel pulls a streamer from her hair. "I could do with less glitter. Let's go find some real food."

❦

It's still early—and even earlier back home—when we finish dinner, but Maribel wants to go back up to our room to lay out her clothes and practice her speech.

I had assumed it would be about Tía Carla. Besides Dad, she's the only businessperson we know. And she's super successful.

Instead, Maribel recites, "She might not be a businesswoman, but if you ask me, there's no one who better embodies the spirit of success than my nana. That's because success begins with recognizing potential, and Nana sees potential almost everywhere she looks."

She rehearses in front of the mirror and twice in front of me before we both collapse on our beds.

"You're sure you don't want to practice?" Maribel mumbles into her pillow. "Just once?"

"No, I just want to get it over with."

"Then do me a favor and toss me my phone so I can set an alarm?"

"We don't need an alarm." I yawn. "I always wake up early on days when something important is supposed to happen."

CHAPTER EIGHTEEN

You can make it, but it's easier if you don't
have to do it alone.
—BETTY FORD

We wake up to sunlight pouring through the gauzy
hotel curtains.

"Geez!" Maribel barks. "What time is it?"

I pat the top of the nightstand until I find my
rose-gold watch where I had taken it off last night.

I hold it a few inches above my nose. "It's okay.
It's only six thirty."

"Oh, good. Wake me up in half an hour." She
pulls a pillow over her face.

But wait.

My watch is still set to California time. I sit up. The hotel clock flashes a scolding 9:31.

"Maribel, get up!" I jump out of bed and tear off her covers. "Get up!"

She pulls the blankets back over her face. "Geez, what are you doing? We have time."

"*No,*" I insist, switching on all the lights. "We don't."

Maribel sits up, shakes her head, and looks at the clock. Then she pulls it off the nightstand for a closer look. "Geez!"

She bolts for the shower and slams the bathroom door.

I've never seen Maribel frazzled before. I'm not sure what to do.

Don't make us any later, I think, and change into my gray skirt and white button-up blouse.

Three minutes later, the shower stops running, and not much longer after that, Maribel pokes her head out the door. "Geez, you can come in here if you need to get ready."

She has toweled off a clear spot in the foggy mirror and is smoothing foundation onto her forehead with a sponge. She dusts rosy blush over her cheeks and nose, then lines her eyelids with a charcoal-colored pencil.

I brush my teeth, then wipe off my own little patch of mirror.

It isn't good.

"Maribel, I need your help."

I slept in my braid, and now my hair is stiff and crinkly. My lips are chapped from the dry hotel air.

"Geez, you look fine," Maribel says, without even glancing at me.

"No." I grab her wrist. "Maribel, *please.*"

"Okay, okay," she says, putting her hairbrush down by the sink. "Sit down."

I hop up on the counter. Maribel puts dots of foundation all over my face, then blends them with her fingers. Next, she swirls a feathery makeup brush in a little container of blush. I sneeze when it flutters over my nose.

She opens a tube of mascara. "Look up."

I try not to blink as she swipes it over my eyelashes.

"All right. Now get down so I can do your hair."

She brushes it smooth, then pulls it into a tight

ponytail high on top of my head. She twists it into a bun and pins back my bangs.

Finally, Maribel steps back, tilts her head, and narrows her eyes, trying to decide what else she should fuss with or fix. "Maybe lipstick?" She rummages through her bag and pulls out a peachy-pink shade. "But not too much."

She dabs it on my lips, rips a scrap of toilet paper off the roll, and hands it to me. "Blot.

"There," she says. "What do you think?"

I turn to the mirror. Even though I've *sold* a lot of makeup, I've never really worn much before. My eyes seem brighter, my cheeks pinker. The foundation covers up all my freckles. I look more like Maribel and more like Mom. But I can't tell whether I look more or less like myself.

"You look beautiful," Maribel says. "Finish getting dressed and meet me in front of the banquet room. Can you find your way? I'm going up now in case they're looking for us." She slips her arms into her plum-colored blazer and flies out the door. I shudder as it slams shut.

There isn't very much left to do. Just put on my lavender cardigan and my new black heels. The sweater is in the closet where I hung it last night. The shoes should be in the front pocket of my suitcase.

Only they aren't.

I reach into the pocket again and take out everything that's inside. No shoes. I dig through the rest of my suitcase, tossing out sweaters and pajamas and jeans.

My palms start to sweat.

I get on the floor and peer under the beds—maybe we kicked them underneath without noticing. I go back to the closet. I check behind the bathroom door. I even empty the wastebaskets. The shoes aren't anywhere.

I know I *must* have packed them; I *had* to have packed them. But when I stop and think about it, I have to admit I can't *remember* packing them. A knot tightens in my stomach.

It's already 10:02. I picture Maribel upstairs, tapping her foot impatiently and wondering what's keeping me. I don't know what else to do, so I put on my sneakers.

Laces tied, I hang my lanyard around my neck and race to the elevator. I press the button for the

211

twelfth floor and hold my breath as the car lurches upward.

The doors open on Maribel, hands on her hips. "What took you so—" She stops when her eyes land on my feet. "Geez! What is going on with your shoes?"

They're more gray than white now. The rubber sole is starting to come apart at the heel of the left one. The yellow-orange ribbons are frayed at both ends.

"These are all I have."

"You have to be kidding."

I shake my head, wishing I were.

"Okay. It's okay. There's nothing we can do about it now. Come on, Mary Ellen is waiting."

Mary Ellen Bloomer is standing outside the banquet hall. The badge around her neck says she's Director of Inspiration, and she looks as if she has been dipped in a giant bucket of purple, from the twinkle of her amethyst earrings to the tips of her eggplant pumps.

"This must be Griselda," she says, opening her arms to envelop me in a berry-scented hug. I

212

pull away and recognize the lollipop shine of Mary Ellen's lip gloss when she smiles. Sugar Plum.

She takes one of my hands and one of Maribel's and looks us over. "Oh!" she says, grimacing when she notices my shoes. "Oh," she says again, composing herself. "Well, let's get the two of you seated. You don't want to miss brunch."

The swirling notes of a piano melody and the low hum of a hundred voices escape from the banquet hall when Mary Ellen opens the doors to lead us in. She steers us to a round table near the front, the only one that still has empty seats.

"Here we are. Now, you just enjoy some breakfast. We'll call your name when it's time for you to come up and give your speech." She whirls around and walks away, lavender scarf flying out behind her.

Maribel smiles at everyone around the table. She pulls out her chair, sits down, shakes out her napkin, and lays it across her lap. Then she holds out her hand and introduces herself to the man on her right.

I just sit and stare at the pitchers of orange juice

and grapefruit juice, and the pretty ceramic tea-pot on the table in front of me. I can't believe we made it.

Maribel reaches over for the orange juice. She pours, still nodding as the man next to her keeps talking.

She offers me the glass.

"OJ, Geez?"

"No, thanks."

"You should eat something," she whispers.

At the center of the table, next to a bowl of sky-blue hydrangeas, is a tray of croissants and scones and tiny muffins—some with blueberries and some freckled with poppy seeds—and a three-tiered tower of fruit, strawberries at the bottom, melon in the middle, and bunches of grapes dripping over the top.

Using silver tongs that look almost doll-size, I drop a muffin on my plate and nibble a bit of the streusel topping.

The piano music fades. Then, table by table, the voices hush, too, until the only sounds are the scraping of forks on plates and the clink of ice in glass pitchers.

"On behalf of Alma Cosmetics, I wish each and every one of you a beautiful morning!"

I turn around and look to the very front of the banquet hall. Mary Ellen is behind a podium onstage speaking into a microphone.

Here we go.

"It is my pleasure to welcome you to our annual Soul of Beauty Brunch. This year, we are especially proud to introduce the finalists in Alma's first-ever Fresh New Face competition, celebrating the launch of our new Fairytale line for teens and tweens. Finalists, will you please stand?"

There are fifteen of us, one or two at each round table. The audience applauds as we scoot back our chairs and stand.

"Look around, ladies and gentlemen, standing in this room, right here, right now, is the fresh new face of Alma Cosmetics."

They clap louder.

"Thank you, ladies. You may sit down. And now I'd like to introduce our panel of judges...."

The woman on my left has billowy brown curls and a name tag that says she's Assistant Regional

Manager of Outreach and Opportunity. She leans toward me.

"Nervous?"

"I guess a little."

"Well, don't be." She squeezes my arm. "I'm sure you'll do fine. Anyway, it's an accomplishment just to have made it this far."

I smile back at her, but all I can think is how awful it would feel to have made it this far and not any farther. To have to face Mom's sad half-smile and Dad's tired voice and tell them that once again we've lost.

I look back up at Mary Ellen, who is still speaking.

"...And who better than our Fresh New Face finalists to tell the story of how Alma opens the doors of entrepreneurship to ambitious young people across the nation? Without further ado, please welcome our first finalist, from Duluth, Minnesota, Miss Audrey Cole."

It's a big room, but it feels stuffy. I want to take off my cardigan, but instead I roll up the sleeves. I can't eat. I can't concentrate on the speeches. I try to go over mine in my head, but I keep stumbling, forgetting the words. I wish I had practiced last night.

I don't notice my foot tapping until Maribel touches my knee to stop it.

"Geez, are you okay? Try to calm down. Here, have some tea."

The teacup has ribbons of gold painted around the top and bottom edges, and between them is a bluebonnet against a field of tiny golden dots. The handle curves gently like a grapevine, only it's so delicate it looks as if it might snap off in my hand if I hold on too tight. The porcelain glows as though, instead of tea inside, there's a candle flickering.

I think of my teacups back home, the ones I always thought were so precious and elegant. I picture them next to the one I'm holding, and all I can see is dull, chipped glaze. I can almost feel the clunky weight of them. They were never really worth anything. They are old, secondhand. Things that other people had thrown away, but that I, for some reason, thought were worth more.

The bluebonnet goes all blurry. I blink hard to stop the tears from spilling down my cheeks and smearing the mascara Maribel has applied. It's not because I'm nervous about speaking. It's because deep down I know that selling every shade of lip gloss won't bring back the sparkle of the way things used to be. Because the way things *really* used to be isn't how I've been remembering them. Everything I thought was storybook perfect was really cracked and breaking. I don't know if five thousand dollars will bring Dad home. It might, but it won't erase everything that's happened. And becoming the fresh new face of Alma Cosmetics won't make me feel like myself again.

Maribel nudges my shoulder. "Geez," she whispers. "Geez, it's your turn."

"What?"

"You have to get up there. She's calling you." She squeezes my hand before I go. "You're fine."

I wind around tables, trying not to look at my feet, but also trying not to think about the hundreds of eyes following me up the steps to the stage.

At least I don't fall down.

I get to the podium and tap the microphone. It crackles.

I clear my throat and try to swallow down the shake I expect to hear in my voice, but when I open my mouth and recite, "Thank you and good morning," there isn't one.

My feet are still. My palms are dry. I know the words I have to say.

"My dad once took a small business and turned it into a big one."

I look to the table of judges. One of them smiles at me and makes a note on the paper in front of her.

"Maybe he didn't become a millionaire, but at least we didn't worry about money."

I look at Maribel. She has turned her chair all the way around so her back is to the table and she's facing me. She's leaning so far forward her necklace skims her kneecaps. She nods at me to keep going.

"Until he lost his business."

Maribel sits all the way back.

"And we lost our house. And a lot of other things, too. My older sister, Maribel, especially. She's supposed to be at college right now. She worked really hard for it. But when she lost the thing she wanted most, she didn't run away, and she didn't pretend everything was all right. She worked even harder to find another way. Maribel is the person who best represents the spirit of success.

She's sitting back there, and she should be the fresh new face of Alma Cosmetics."

My nerves catch up to me, and so do my tears, and this time I can't blink them away. I'm down the stairs and out the door before Mary Ellen can introduce the next finalist.

CHAPTER NINETEEN

You may not always have a comfortable life,
and you will not always be able to solve all of
the world's problems at once, but don't ever
underestimate the importance you can have
because history has shown us that courage
can be contagious and hope can take on a life
of its own.

—Michelle Obama

I make it all the way back to our room before I remember that Maribel has the key card. Figures.

I slide down the wall and onto the floor. The carpet in the hallway is cranberry-colored, and the walls are drab beige. It's hard to believe I'm still on the same planet, let alone in the same building, as the purple explosion upstairs in the banquet hall.

Maybe it wasn't all for nothing. When we fly home tomorrow, Mom and I will still be living in Nana's house. Dad will still be living someplace else. His truck will still be stuck at the mechanic's. But maybe Maribel will be on her way to college again. She's probably giving her speech right now. Unstoppable as always.

But she isn't giving her speech. She's on her way down the hall. I'd recognize her quick, sure foot-steps anywhere.

"Oh, Geez." She drops her satchel and slides down next to me. "That was some speech."

"How did yours go?"

"Oh, they ate it up."

"Good."

"Or, at least, they would have if I'd given it. It was a pretty good speech, you know."

"Mari!" I look up from the carpet to face her. "You didn't give your speech?"

"I wasn't going to just let you run off by your-self. I would have been up here sooner if Mary

Ellen hadn't kept me down there to explain what in the world you were talking about."

"So I ruined it for both of us. Great."

"Five thousand dollars would have been nice, but I didn't really want to be the fresh new face of Alma Cosmetics. I mean, did you?"

"No. But now you won't be able to move out and go to college."

"I'll go. Maybe not as soon as I wanted, but I'll go."

To anyone else listening, her voice might seem only a little bit quiet, just barely sad. To me, it sounds like something about to crumble. Like a crack spreading across fine porcelain.

But her face is a cool, half-smiling mask.

"So," she continues. "We're going to need to do something about Mom's old curtains. I think I've seen enough purple over the past two days to last the rest of my life."

She pulls her lanyard with her name badge over her head and then takes mine, too.

"Maribel, stop."

I check my watch.

"You should go back down there. The brunch isn't over yet. I'm sure Mary Ellen would still let you give your speech. You could still win."

"Better idea." She stands up, unlocks the door, and nudges it open with her hip. "Get your coat."

⌒⌒

The elevator doors open up onto the lobby with a friendly ding. Maribel strides out and heads straight for the concierge.

He flashes a smile as cheerful as a field of sunflowers. He'd make a great Alma Cosmetics salesman. "Good morning, ladies. Can I help you arrange a tour? Or maybe you'd like a recommendation for lunch?"

Except for that nibble of blueberry muffin, I haven't eaten all morning. "Actually, food sounds—"

"No, thanks," Maribel says. "We already have plans. I just need a couple of these."

She scans the maps on his desk, grabs two, and spins around toward the hotel's revolving door.

"But, Maribel, where are we going?"

She doesn't stop.

I blink as we pass from the soft hotel light out

into the bright late-morning glare. The first deep breath of cold air makes me cough, but the breeze against my cheeks is a refreshing change from the stale warmth inside. I flip the collar of my new wool coat up so it covers my neck.

Maribel is already halfway down the block. I see the purple scarf still tied to her bag. I jog after her.

"Maribel, slow down!"

"Walk faster," she says. "It's freezing."

I catch up with her at the corner. While we wait for the signal to change, Maribel unfolds one of the maps, then looks up at the street sign. A double-decker tour bus lumbers past. I pull my hands back into the sleeves of my coat and shiver. "You still haven't told me where we're going."

She folds up the map and tucks it into her makeup bag.

"That's because it's a surprise."

We come to a long carpet of grass stretching left and right in front of us and finally stop for a break. The lawn is yellow and patchy in places, damaged by the winter cold. The trees are still bare, but soon new green leaves will unfurl on their branches. Maribel dodges a soccer ball that comes flying toward us while we wait for our order at a hot dog cart.

At one end of the lawn, the dome of the Capitol Building looms stark white against the blue sky. So far away, it still looks like a picture on a postcard or in one of my schoolbooks. I remember what Mrs. Ramos-McCaffrey said about how our history books are filled with the stories of ordinary people, and I think about how different my story is from what I expected.

After we finish eating, Maribel leads us toward the towering Washington Monument at the other end of the National Mall. Tourists crowd around its base, aiming their cameras up, up, up.

"Is this where you're taking us?"

We still don't stop. Maribel walks a little farther down a paved walkway and across a busy street.

"*Now* can you tell me where we're going?"

"Geez, you don't give up, do you? Relax. We're almost there."

Finally, she stops. We are near the edge of what appears to be a lake. Maribel looks around. She scrunches up her nose and takes a pamphlet out of her bag.

She glances down at the pamphlet, then out at the dirt.

"It should be right here."

"What should be right here?"

"Something called the Floral Library."

I look harder and can just make out the edges of flower beds.

"There's supposed to be 'ten thousand tulip bulbs to fill the library's ninety-three beds,'" Maribel reads. "I saw the brochure when we were waiting for the keys to our hotel room. I thought, if we had time, you would want to see it, but..."

"But tulips don't bloom until spring!" I burst into laughter. "This pile of dirt? That's the big surprise?"

"Oh. *Geez!*" Maribel shouts. A man in an olive National Park Service uniform turns around and looks at us. She lowers her voice. "I don't mean you, Geez. I mean, *geez*, I didn't think anything else could possibly go wrong today."

I cannot stop giggling. "You thought there would be tulips? In *February*?"

She's shaking her head, but she has started

laughing, too. She socks me playfully on the shoulder.

"Quit laughing. You're the garden expert, not me."

"No kidding." I snatch the brochure from her hand. "Let me see that."

The Floral Library—also known as the Tulip Library—was created in 1969 as part of Lady Bird Johnson's Capital Beautification Project. Each fall, National Park Service gardeners plant 10,000 tulip bulbs to fill the library's 93 beds.

Under the words is a picture of Lady Bird Johnson. She has one foot on the ground and one resting on top of the blade of a shovel, about to plunge it into the dirt. She isn't wearing her yellow ballgown, but work clothes. Gardening clothes: a cowboy hat and checkered shirt, the kind Nana wears all the time.

I fold the brochure and put it in my coat pocket. It's more than just a pile of dirt. So much more. The beds in front of us only look empty because the flowers are still hidden underground. I can imagine them blooming, pink and yellow and orange and red. Already, the green tips of a few eager shoots are sprouting up from the soil. Ten thousand bulbs. Year after year, someone has to kneel down on the ground, dig into the dirt, and replant them, trusting that after every winter, the flowers will come back. Not exactly the way they were before, but still beautiful.

"I'm so sorry, Griselda."

I like the sound of my name when she says it. A fighter.

"Don't be sorry. I'm glad we came."

C—ɔ

There is a mirror hanging in the hotel lobby, and I catch our reflection as we walk past on our way to the elevators. We definitely don't look like the fresh new faces of anything. Maribel is carrying her shoes after kicking them off the second we stepped through the revolving doors. My shoes are damp and even grayer than they were this morning. Our cheeks are pink and our hair is frizzy.

I remember the mirrors in Tía Carla's salon. How if you stand in just the right spot, you can see a dozen different versions of yourself staring back. But what version will I see the next time I'm there?

The version of me who lived in my old house is gone. And so is the version who couldn't do anything on her own—not even let herself out of a bathroom stall.

But the version who can plant beautiful things and make them grow is still here.

When we get to our hotel room, we find a gift basket wrapped in cellophane and topped with a satin bow. Taped to the front is a little envelope with my name on it.

"Who's it from?" Maribel asks.

"Don't know."

Inside the envelope is a notecard with a bouquet of violets printed on the front and in gold letters along the bottom, *The Soul of Beauty.*

I open the card and read it aloud.

Dear Miss Griselda Zaragoza,
    We truly appreciate the talent, hard work, and dedication you put into Alma's Fresh New Face Challenge. Although you were not selected as the Fresh New Face of Alma Cosmetics, we are proud of your accomplishments

and you should be, too. We hope you will consider opportunities with Alma as you continue to pursue your goals.

Please accept this gift as a token of our friendship.

At the bottom of the card, in curling hand-written letters, is written **Wishing you a beautiful future. Yours sincerely, Mary Ellen Bloomer.**

"I guess that makes it official. I lost." I lift up the basket to take it to my bed. Underneath is an envelope for Maribel.

"Hey, they left something for you, too."

"But no gift basket. I guess you had to actually give your speech to get one of those."

"Don't you want to see what it says?"

"Why not?" She tears open the envelope. I watch her face as she reads.

Eyebrows wrinkle. Eyes widen. A gasp.

She flips over the letter to see if there's anything on the back. The other side is blank, so she flips it back over and reads again.

"Oh, my gosh."

"What is it?"

"Is this for real?"

"Maribel. *Tell* me."

She reads: "'Dear Miss Maribel Zaragoza,' *blah, blah, blah,* you didn't win the contest, fresh new face, etcetera. Okay. Here's the good part: 'We at Alma Cosmetics believe that opportunity is the seed of success. Based on your tenacity and entrepreneurial spirit, we are pleased to offer you an academic scholarship, renewable annually for as long as you are a full-time student in good standing at an institution of higher education.'"

It's not the grand prize, but I know what a scholarship means: maybe a new way for Maribel.

"Is it enough? Does this mean you get to go?"

"With what I've saved so far? I'm a lot closer than I was before."

I make her read it again. The words sound like magic. They sparkle. They sound like Once Upon a Time and Happily Ever After all swirled together.

"You should call Mom. And Dad."

"In a minute. Hey, Geez?"

"Yeah?"

"Thank you." She holds the letter over her heart. Her eyes glisten, and I think she might cry. But she's still Maribel. She blinks once and it's gone. "Now, are you going to open that basket or what? Seriously, you're worse than Nana."

I untie the ribbon and peel apart the cellophane. The basket holds dozens of Alma samples: moisturizer, lipstick, eye shadow, blush. It reminds me of a piñata from the birthday parties we used to have in our old backyard—and even more so when Maribel turns the basket upside down and dumps it out onto her bed.

She picks out a moss-green eye shadow. "Ah," she says. "Close your eyes, and in no time, Alma will have you looking as wicked as a witch." She pops open the little container. I scoot over to let her brush the makeup over my eyelids.

"I feel more wicked already." I flutter my eyes. Then I dig through the pile of samples and pull out a shimmery bronzer. "Your turn." Maribel leans in. "Just a little bit of this, and you'll be as dazzling as a disco ball."

CHAPTER TWENTY

Where flowers bloom, so does hope.

—Lady Bird Johnson

Mom is waiting for us at the bottom of an airport escalator after our flight lands in California on Sunday afternoon. She's pointing her cell-phone camera at us. Maribel and I look at each other.

"What do you think she's doing?" I ask.

"No idea."

When we get to the bottom, Maribel complains, "Mom, *please*. We've been on an airplane for, like, six hours. I look like a zombie."

"Oh, stop," Mom says, still recording.

She takes a step toward Maribel and slips into her reporter's voice. "Tell me, Miss Zaragoza, how does it feel to be the newest recipient of Alma's Soul of Opportunity Scholarship?"

"Ugh." Maribel pulls the hood of her sweatshirt over her face.

"All right, all right," Mom says in her usual voice, and lowers the phone so she can hug us. "I missed you two so much this weekend, I started watching home movies. And *then* I realized how long it's been since I've gotten you girls on video."

"We were only gone for two days," I say. "You couldn't have missed us that much."

She puts one arm around my shoulders and one around Maribel's, and we walk clumsily toward the luggage carousels to pick up our bags.

"Of course I missed you. It doesn't feel like home without you. Speaking of home, remember to call your dad when we get there. I'm sure he wants to hear all about your trip."

An hour later, we park in Nana's driveway. Yet another toilet is sitting on the lawn.

"Where'd that one come from?"

"A neighbor? A garage sale? I don't know, it just appeared this morning." Mom shakes her head. "You know how Nana is. There's no stopping her."

"It's not so bad," I say, opening the trunk to take out my suitcase. "I was just wondering if she knows what she's going to plant in this one."

After I empty my suitcase and start a load of laundry, I call my dad like Mom suggested, only it's not the trip I want to talk to him about.

"I've been thinking about the mint problem."

"Have you?"

"We could smother it like we did our old lawn, but digging it up would probably be faster. Either way, we have to get rid of it or nothing else will be able to grow. Only, Nana won't want to get rid of *all* of it."

Dad is quiet for a few seconds. Then he says, "You could try replanting some of it in a pot or container. That way, she'll still have the mint, but it won't grow so out of control again."

"That's exactly what I was thinking." And I know just the container we can use. It is sitting on Nana's lawn, never to be flushed again.

"Maybe this weekend, or the weekend after, I can drive up there. If you want some help with it?"

I think about it. "You should come March third," I tell him. "There's this thing at school I want you to see."

We say goodbye, and I carry my suitcase back to the bedroom.

My new black heels are in their box next to the nightstand. All the clothes I didn't take to Washington, DC, are still piled on the bed. Normally, I'd put them back in the suitcase. But this time, I fold the T-shirts and match the socks and put them away in the drawers Maribel left empty for me when we first moved in. I borrow some hangers from her side of the closet and get to work on my jeans and dresses.

⌒

Mom says I can stay home from school on Monday to catch up on sleep, but I want to go. I even wake up before the alarm clock starts bleeping.

Maribel is at the kitchen table, dunking the end of a gingerbread pig into her cup of coffee and working on a crossword puzzle with Nana. Her makeup satchel is on the floor next to her chair.

I pour myself a bowl of cereal and sit next to her. "Give me a ride to school, since you're up?"

Maribel swallows the last bite of gingerbread and shakes the crumbs off her fingers. "Sorry, Geez," she says. "I'm on my way out. Alma appointment. Those college books aren't going to buy themselves."

Mom walks into the kitchen with a gray suit jacket draped over her arm. "I can drop you off."

"Aren't you on your way to Tía Carla's?"

"No," she says, leaning over Nana's shoulder to grab a piece of pumpkin empanada. "I'm going to your school for a few hours this morning."

"What for?" I hope it's not another trip to Dr. Keckley's office.

"Mr. Singh asked me to come visit with his journalism class. I'm going to help them out with a little videography project. No big deal. Should be fun, though."

Maribel picks up her bag, reaches in, and takes out a tube of lip gloss. Carnation pink with flecks of gold.

"Here you go, Mom. Flatters everyone."

"Just what I needed." She kisses the top of Maribel's head.

I finish breakfast and get ready for school. One

last time, I zip a few Alma boxes into my backpack, hug Nana, and meet Mom out in the driveway.

$$\mathcal{C}\mathbin{\raisebox{0.3ex}{\scriptsize$\sim$}}$$

Sophia is sitting three tables away with Daisy.

I check my watch again. Only five minutes left until lunch break is over, and I still haven't talked to her.

"Geez, just go over there already," Logan says. "What's the worst she could say? You're still friends, right?"

I think so. But I don't know for sure, and I'm afraid to find out.

"Just *go* and get it over with. This is so boring."

"Okay, okay, I'm going."

I take my backpack and walk over to her table. "Hey, Daisy. Hey, Sophia."

"Geez. You're back." She says it as if I missed weeks of school instead of just one day.

I take the boxes out of my backpack. "I have some things for you."

Her forehead wrinkles. "Not more makeup?"

"Sort of, but not exactly. You might actually like this stuff." First, I give her a sample of sunscreen from Alma's Overprotective line. "So your nose doesn't get so burnt next summer."

Next, a trial-size bottle of Clean as Crystal clarifying shampoo. "It's supposed to keep your hair from turning colors after swimming. I thought you could try it. I mean, not that chlorine hair looks bad or anything."

She grabs the bottle. "No, I hate having chlorine hair, and I've tried *everything*."

Last, a tube of lip gloss. "The color is called Red Riding Hood. It's for your Rita Moreno costume. I looked up a picture of her. I think this is the perfect shade."

That was the easy part. I wish I could just stop there. But I remember something Lady Bird Johnson once said: "The way you overcome shyness is to become so wrapped up in something that you forget to be afraid." It worked at the Alma Expo, so maybe it'll work in the school cafeteria. I make myself keep going. I try to forget to be afraid.

"I'm sorry for snapping at you. I should have just told you about Dad and the house and everything. I was just scared. And sort of embarrassed."

"No, *I'm* sorry. I felt so stupid afterward, and I didn't know what to say to you."

"Do you think your mom would let you come over after school? I'm working on a project and I need some help."

She doesn't answer right away. Maybe she already has plans with her other friends. Or maybe she feels weird about coming to Nana's.

She squeals and claps her hands. "Yes! I'll ask my mom when she picks up Lucas."

$\sim$

Sophia hung out in my room—my old room— millions of times before. But this is the first time anyone besides my family has seen my new room, the one I'm sharing with Maribel.

I stop in the hallway, take a deep breath, and open the door.

"This is it."

"It's nice," Sophia says, running her fingers over the daisy-chain wallpaper. "But why is it so empty? Where's all your stuff? It almost looks like you don't really live here."

I don't, I almost say. But I stop myself. I do live here, and that's part of my story now, too.

"That's what I need help with."

I had gotten the idea from the toilets.

I take the Lady Bird Johnson teacup off my windowsill, and dump the loose change onto the desk. Then I reach under my bed for the rest of the collection. "Let's go."

I carry the box to the backyard and set it down on the grass. Sophia lifts a corner and peeks inside. "All your teacups?"

I take one of them out of the box, carefully unroll the bubble wrap, and set it aside. Sophia starts popping it between her fingers. "I love this stuff."

I turn the cup around in my hand. Frances Cleveland. It's white with a red band painted along the top. A wreath of orange blossoms and laurel leaves frames her portrait.

The next cup is pale blue with a bouquet of white dogwood at the center. Edith Wilson.

As we unpack the teacups and line them up on the grass, I hear Ms. Johnson's car, and then the *ba-bump, ba-bump* of Logan's handball bouncing off the driveway and against the garage door.

"Be right back," I tell Sophia, and jog to the front yard. "Hey!" I call.

Logan catches the ball after the next bounce. "Hey."

"Sophia and I are working on something. Do you want to come over and help?"

He rolls the ball back to his porch and follows me.

While Sophia and Logan unwrap the rest of the teacups, I go into the garage. There's another box I need to find.

Most of the stuff in there is Nana's—not-quite-empty paint buckets, Christmas ornaments in clear plastic bins, old furniture that she doesn't want in the house anymore but also doesn't want to throw away.

The boxes from our old house are all stored in the same corner, one labeled OFFICE and another KITCHEN. There is a pile of Maribel's high school textbooks and trophies, and a lumpy trash bag that's filled with my old stuffed animals. Next to the bag is the box I'm looking for: GARDEN.

I slice open the packing tape with the edge of a screwdriver and start searching. My hand shovel and trowel are on top. I set those aside. We might need them later. I find dozens of seed packets and a bag of Spanish moss.

I keep digging, all the way down to the bottom of the box, until I get to the summer-blooming bulbs I wrapped up in dishtowels: ranunculus, dahlia, and begonia.

It's after the last freeze now. The timing should be just right.

I hold the bulbs and hand shovel under my arm and drag a bag of Nana's potting soil to Sophia and Logan. I sit down between them and spread the bulbs out on the lawn. Sophia pokes at a ranunculus with a twig. It looks a little like a brown crab with fat, wriggling legs. But it will grow into a flower as vivid as the sunset.

Logan picks up three begonia bulbs and tries to juggle them. They look like dirt clods now, but someday they will open up red and frilly and full of joy.

I choose one of the dahlias.

"Is it...a potato?" Sophia asks.

"No, it's not a potato." I laugh and show them what to do next. I use the hand shovel to scoop soil into one of the teacups. With my finger, I hollow out a shallow hole, press the bulb inside, and then cover it with dirt.

It's hard to tell right now, but buried underneath is the promise of something beautiful getting ready to grow.

ACKNOWLEDGMENTS

To Stockton, a city full of strivers: I am so grateful to know you.

To my agent, Jennifer Laughran; editor, Nikki Garcia; and everyone at Little, Brown, especially Marcie Lawrence, Annie McDonnell, Erika Schwartz, Kristina Pisciotta, and Jennifer Poe; to Christian Burkin and Paula Sheil; and, as always, to David, Alice, and Soledad: love and muchas gracias.